BAD NEWS

Stevie and Phil returned to Pine Hollow as quickly as possible. In less than ten minutes, the stable was in sight.

That was when Stevie started getting worried, for she could see Carole and Lisa in the field at the back of the stable, perched on the fences. As soon as they spotted Stevie and Phil, they began waving. It wasn't a greeting, it was a hurry-up wave. Stevie nudged Topside and got him to quicken his gait. She felt a little knot tighten in her stomach. Something was wrong, and the closer she got to Pine Hollow, the surer she was something was really wrong and it had to do with her. . . .

The Saddle Club series by Bonnie Bryant; ask your bookseller for
titles you have missed:

THE SADDLE CLUB

CHOCOLATE HORSE

BONNIE BRYANT

BANTAM BOOKS
TORONTO · NEW YORK · LONDON · SYDNEY · AUCKLAND

I would like to express special thanks to
Dr. Peter Zeale and Mary Gina Stilwell,
who helped me with this book.

BB

THE SADDLE CLUB: CHOCOLATE HORSE
A BANTAM BOOK 0 553 40761 9

First published in USA by Bantam Skylark Books
First publication in Great Britain

PRINTING HISTORY
Bantam edition published 1994

With thanks to Chris and Sam of Coltspring Riding School for their
help in the preparation of the cover

Bantam Books are published by Transworld Publishers Ltd,
61–63 Uxbridge Road, Ealing, London W5 5SA, in Australia by
Transworld Publishers (Australia) Pty Ltd, 15–25 Helles Avenue,
Moorebank, NSW 2170, and in New Zealand by Transworld
Publishers (NZ) Ltd, 3 William Pickering Drive, Albany, Auckland.

Printed and bound in Great Britain by
Cox & Wyman Ltd, Reading, Berks.

For Craig Virden, a true chocolate-lover,
who inspired this book and this story.

"LET ME JUST say one more good-bye to Starlight," Carole Hanson said to her two best friends, Stevie Lake and Lisa Atwood.

"Sure," Stevie agreed. "You won't be seeing him for another full day, will you?" She was teasing and Carole knew it.

"If Starlight were your horse, you'd be doing the same thing, wouldn't you?" Carole asked, giving the horse a final farewell hug.

Stevie smiled because Carole was right, and just to show there were no hard feelings, she gave Starlight a hug, too. He liked the attention. The girls liked giving it to him.

The girls had just finished their Tuesday riding class at Pine Hollow. They had a class every Tuesday, and their Pony Club, named Horse Wise, met on Saturdays. Since twice a week wasn't anywhere near enough horses for the three horse-crazy girls, they tried to get to Pine Hollow almost every day. When they couldn't ride, they could just talk about horses, and there were always chores to do around the stable. The stable owner, Max Regnery, and his mother, affectionately called Mrs. Reg by all the riders, encouraged everyone to pitch in at Pine Hollow. "Encouraged" wasn't the word they usually used, though. "Insisted" was more like it.

The girls didn't mind. They were so horse crazy that they'd do anything to be around horses, and when they weren't around horses, they talked about them. They called that having a Saddle Club meeting. The three of them had formed the club, and it had only two rules. Members had to be horse crazy, and they had to be willing to help one another out. They were such good friends that they never had trouble following either of those rules.

Stevie slung her book bag over her shoulder, grimacing under the weight, and then followed her friends out the stable door. It was time to get home; she had a lot of homework. She'd do it, too, but not because she liked doing it. She knew that if her grades slipped, Max wouldn't let her ride. He insisted that his riders maintain a satisfactory grade average. Stevie's grade average hovered perilously close to Max's idea of satisfactory. At the moment she was in hot water because two of her math assignments had mysteriously disappeared somewhere between her desk and her teacher's desk. Her teacher wasn't happy about it and refused to believe that Stevie's cat, Madonna, had eaten the homework.

"Cats don't like prealgebra," Miss Snyder had said. Stevie had resisted the impulse to add that she didn't either.

"So what are you going to wear to the dance?" Lisa asked, bringing Stevie's attention to a more fun subject. Valentine's Day was just a week and a half away, and Pine Hollow was celebrating the event by holding a barn dance for its young riders.

Lisa was the most clothes conscious of the three girls, always perfectly turned out. Stevie favored casual clothes—jeans and turtlenecks. Carole never much cared what she wore as long as she could ride horses in it.

"I guess as long as it's a barn dance, I'll wear my jeans," Stevie said. "And I have a cowboy shirt and my cowboy boots. How's that?"

"Sounds perfect," Lisa said. It wasn't often that she totally agreed with Stevie's wardrobe. "Your boots are really nice, too. I remember you bought them before you and Carole went out West last summer."

"Yup, and they got scuffed up, too, and that's a good thing, because there's nothing worse than looking like a dude—with shiny boots."

Carole beamed at her friends. "Have you ever noticed that even when we're talking about clothes, we're still talking about horses?" Stevie and Lisa grinned. That was the kind of thing that made The Saddle Club special to its members.

Stevie's house was the closest to Pine Hollow, and when the three of them reached it, she said good-bye to her friends, and the Saddle Club meeting ended. They promised they'd talk later that night. Stevie waved and went into the house.

She paused on her way through the family room, shrugging off her coat and her backpack. Her mind was not on those things, though. All she could see was the box of tissues next to the most comfortable chair. That reminded her that her twin brother Alex had stayed home from school today. The lucky guy. He'd claimed he had a cold. Since Stevie's day at school had been especially rotten, it didn't seem fair that Alex had had a nice quiet day at home—watching game shows and soap operas.

Stevie grumbled jealously. "He probably spent the

rest of the day copying the math homework he stole from me that Miss Snyder was so upset about." Only her cat heard her say that.

"Stevie, don't drop your backpack on the floor and don't forget to hang up your coat," her mother called from her home office. Stevie picked up the backpack and the coat, barely registering the fact that her mother's admonition had been delivered from a place where she could not have seen the coat and the backpack on the floor. She just *knew*.

Stevie stomped upstairs. She wished she could get a cold and stay home, too. In fact, it might be a good idea to get a cold on Thursday morning, because she had a history test that day. It was on the Spanish Armada, and it still wasn't clear to her how a bunch of fishing boats could possibly overthrow a gigantic navy. Her teacher, Mr. Thiele, seemed to think it was very important, though.

The door to Stevie's room was ajar. That was odd. It was usually open wide when she wasn't there, or else closed completely. The fact that it was neither of those seemed suspicious to Stevie. She slowed down as she approached the door and peered in.

Alex was in her room. He was wearing his pajamas—in his case that meant a pair of sweatpants—and he was holding something in his hand.

5

"What have you got?" she demanded, storming into the room.

Alex spun around in surprise. He looked pale, and to Stevie that meant guilty. She'd caught him in the act. In his hands he held a gold-foil-covered chocolate horse. She'd bought it at the mall one day when she'd been looking for a birthday present for Carole. She'd thought it was really pretty and liked having it in her room. She'd never thought of eating it. Alex, however, clearly *had* thought of eating it.

The wrapper was torn on one of the horse's forelegs.

"What are you doing with that?" Stevie asked angrily.

"I just wanted—my throat's so sore and I've got a headache and, well—I thought maybe some chocolate would help," Alex stammered meekly.

"Well, just think again," Stevie said. She marched forward and grabbed the horse out of Alex's hand. She was outraged when she discovered that the horse's leg was broken, and she was going to tell Alex exactly what she thought about what he'd done, but she found that he'd fled to his room. She marched across the hall and flung his door open.

"Just because you can find some excuse not to go to school doesn't mean you're going to get any sympathy from me! And don't try to come up with any more lame excuses about stealing my things. That horse was mine —not yours! You had no right—"

Stevie was just warming up to her lecture about property rights and respect for others' belongings (it was a lecture she could deliver well, because it had been delivered to her many times) when she noticed that Alex was behaving peculiarly. Instead of standing up to her as he usually did, he just backed down, literally, sitting on his bed, then lying down and pulling the covers up. His eyes closed.

Stevie was so astonished, she didn't know what to do. He wasn't going to yell back, or make fun of her?

"I'll get back at you," she went on, but with Alex just lying there, her heart wasn't in it anymore.

She spun on her heel and strode back into her room. He could hide under the covers if he wanted. In the meantime she had to find a way to fix the horse's leg.

Stevie decided to use a toothpick for a splint. She got a box of them from the kitchen and began the painstaking job of inserting toothpicks into the sun-softened chocolate. When the leg was as straight as Stevie thought it was going to get, she carefully rewrapped it in the gold foil and put it back on her windowsill. It tilted to the right. She adjusted it. It listed to the left. Then it

7

occurred to her that she could do a leg wrap on it, the same way she would with a real horse whose leg had gotten wounded.

She hunted through all her desk drawers until she found a tape dispenser that had a note on it reading: "This Belongs to Mom! Do Not Touch! Do Not Borrow! This Means YOU, Stevie!" Stevie carefully pulled out a length of tape and wrapped the horse's leg. It worked well enough for the horse to be able to stand.

She stuck the tape back in her drawer, considered returning the toothpicks to the kitchen but rejected the notion, at least until dinnertime, and settled on her bed, using her backpack filled with undone homework assignments as a prop for her feet. She knew she had to do some work, but she also had some thinking to do. The subject was revenge.

The phone rang, interrupting her thoughts. It was Phil Marsten.

Phil was Stevie's boyfriend. He lived a couple of towns away, so they didn't get to see one another very often, but they did get to talk on the phone quite a bit. It was one of Stevie's favorite things to do.

"Hi there!" he greeted her cheerfully.

"What are you so happy about?" Stevie asked.

"I've got some good news," he said.

"I could use some of that."

"Well, here it is, then: How'd you like to do something together tomorrow afternoon?"

"Really?" Stevie asked, sitting up straight. This sounded as if it were good news.

"Really," Phil said. "My mother has an errand in Willow Creek—something to do with a committee for something or other—and she said she'd bring me over after school and drop me off at your house if you're going to be free. Are you?"

Was she? Stevie thought about it for a while, perhaps a quarter of a second, and then told Phil she definitely *was* free. Then, when she thought about it for another quarter of a second, she realized that she'd rather see Phil someplace where her three brothers weren't, especially if Alex was still able to convince their parents that he was sick. All she needed was a twin brother wandering around in his sweatpants when Phil was there.

"Why don't we meet at Pine Hollow instead—and, like, maybe go for a ride?"

"That's just what I was hoping you'd want to do," Phil said. "Will it be okay with Max?"

"Sure," said Stevie. "He knows you're a good rider, and he'll be glad to let you take one of the horses out.

I'll get there first and arrange it all with Mrs. Reg or Max or whoever's there. How long have we got?"

It turned out that Phil expected to arrive about three-thirty, and his mother would pick him up at five-thirty. That was a perfect amount of time to tack up, go for a ride, bring the horses back, untack, and groom them.

"We can go by the creek. It's so pretty there this time of year," Stevie suggested.

"Wherever you want to go, we'll go," said Phil. "Say, how are plans coming for the dance?" he asked.

That question reminded Stevie of two things: first, that she'd be seeing Phil again in just a week and a half. The second thing was that she'd promised Carole and Lisa that they'd do some work on the decorations for the dance the next day. Now, here she'd gone and promised Phil that they could go for a ride. If she'd thought about Phil's invitation for more than half a second, she would have remembered that before she'd answered. Still, she didn't get many opportunities to see Phil, and she thought her friends would understand. It wasn't as if they were going to be putting up the decorations yet. They were just going to *think* about what they were going to put up. That could wait another day or two, she was sure.

"The plans are coming fine," Stevie said. "In fact, I think the whole thing is going to be just about perfect."

"It always is when you, Carole, and Lisa put your heads together to do something."

Stevie was glad that Phil had such confidence in them, because that was exactly the way she felt about The Saddle Club. Its members seemed to have an infinite ability to solve problems.

"Phil's here," Lisa announced, looking over Stevie's shoulder through the dingy window in Topside's stall. Stevie felt a little chill, a nice little chill. She always liked seeing Phil, and this was no exception. She gave Topside a pat, tugged once more on his girth, pulling it one notch tighter, and went to greet Phil. Lisa brought Topside out of his stall. Carole finished tacking up Barq for Phil and led him out of his stall as well. The girls took the horses into one of Pine Hollow's rings, ready for Stevie and Phil to take their ride.

"How's it going, fellow club members?" Phil asked Lisa and Carole cheerfully. Technically Phil was also a member of The Saddle Club—they called him one of the out-of-town members—and he was always a welcome addition.

"Just fine," Lisa responded. "We'll even survive having the chairperson of our decorating committee miss the first meeting in order to take a ride with you."

"Miss a meeting on my behalf?" Phil asked. "You don't have to do that, Stevie. We can stay here and plan with Lisa and Carole. I've got some great ideas for decorations. You start with crepe paper and some chicken wire, you see—"

"I'm sure they'll do just fine without us," Stevie said. The last thing in the world she wanted was to miss the chance to take a ride with Phil in order to talk about crepe paper and chicken wire.

"No problem," Carole assured him. She'd seen the moment of panic in Stevie's face. "We're just going to take some measurements today to figure out how much crepe paper we'll need. Two can do that as easily as three. Go already."

"If you insist," Phil said.

"I do," said Stevie. That was enough for him. Lisa told her where she and Carole had put the horses. It was time to go.

Phil had been to Pine Hollow many times and was familiar with the horses and even some of the traditions. As soon as he was settled into Barq's saddle, he returned to the stable entrance and touched the good-luck horseshoe. That was something all riders at Pine Hollow did every time they rode. Stevie was there right after Phil. Nobody was sure what the magic was, but they knew it was true. No rider who'd touched the horseshoe had ever gotten seriously injured. Some of the riders suspected the horseshoe was as much a reminder of safe riding habits as it was a talisman. Whatever the case, it worked.

"Let's go," Stevie said. "I'll lead the way."

"You always do," Phil said. Stevie winked at him, clucked her tongue, nudged Topside, and their ride began.

It was a warm February afternoon. The sun shone brightly, heating the dry winter grass and softening the earth below. Stevie found herself keenly aware of everything around her. She could smell the fresh promise of spring and feel the gentle breeze on her cheek. She loved the sound of the horses' hooves rustling the grass as they walked, and then striking the turf sharply when they trotted. She could sense Barq and Phil behind her and Topside below her. She felt very alive and very happy. All thoughts of pesky brothers and missing math assignments fled from her. All she felt was the joy of doing something she loved with someone very special to her.

14

Stevie paused to open a gate, unhitching it with her riding crop, held it open while Phil came through, and then swung it closed with a flick of her ankle. It clicked securely.

"This field's smooth as can be," Stevie said. "Want to canter?"

"Of course," he said. They both knew that they had to choose a place to canter very carefully, especially in the wintertime when the ground might be frozen. But that wasn't the case today. The ground was soft, and Stevie knew that this farmer kept his field free of rocks that might hurt a horse's hooves. They could canter freely all the way across it.

"Race you," Stevie said.

"You're on."

Topside heard the word before he felt her signal to him. He burst into a canter instantly, rocking gently as he propelled forward. Stevie loved this motion of the three-beat gait that Topside did so well, so smoothly and, most important, so quickly.

Topside had a long, smooth stride, and within seconds he'd taken a commanding lead. Stevie glanced over her shoulder and saw the look of determination on Phil's face. He wanted to win just as much as she did and wouldn't think of complaining about the fact that Stevie had gotten a head start when Topside jumped the gun. In fact, winning in spite of that would be an even greater victory.

All thoughts of anything except winning left their minds. The two of them concentrated totally on their goal, the fence at the far side of the field. Stevie leaned forward to reduce wind resistance, and because it gave her the opportunity to whisper important things to Topside.

"We're not going to let him win, are we? There's an extra ration of oats in it for you. Sweet, delicious oats. And a carrot. And maybe an apple. Dipped in molasses."

The list seemed to inspire Topside. He moved faster. But so did Barq. Phil was a very good rider, and he knew how to get the best out of his horse. Stevie could hear them nearing her horse's rear. She could also see that they were approaching the fence.

"A sugar lump!" she whispered triumphantly. It was just enough to inspire a final spurt from Topside. They reached the fence a split second before Phil and Barq.

"Nice race!" Phil said generously.

Stevie shrugged. "Topside started a little early. I'm sure you would have won if he hadn't cheated."

"Maybe," Phil conceded.

The two of them smiled at one another. They were both naturally competitive people, and competition had almost ruined their friendship more than once. They'd learned to be careful.

Stevie opened the gate and then closed it as the two of them walked their horses into the woods. They knew where they were going. There was a path in the woods that led right up to the banks of Willow Creek. There were tree branches where they could secure the horses, and some nice rocks where they could sit and rest and talk. In the summertime riders could take off their boots and dangle their toes in the stream, but that was a few months off yet.

Stevie and Phil dismounted. Phil took Topside's reins as well as Barq's and tied them onto low-hanging branches. Then he joined Stevie by the creek. She was testing the water with her fingers. That confirmed her suspicions that she'd be pushing the season if she took her boots off. The water was icy.

"How's Alex doing?" Phil asked, settling down beside her.

"Fine," Stevie said. "He's missed two days of school now. I'd be doing fine if I'd missed two days of school, too. The only thing I'm worried about is getting his cold. At first I thought he was faking it, but he does seem sort of sick and I don't want to miss the dance next week. But don't worry. Nothing will keep me from it."

"I'm glad about that," Phil said. He took her hand. "I wouldn't want you to miss it, because I think it's going to be a lot of fun. You know, Valentine's Day and all." He gave her hand a little squeeze. She squeezed back.

"Yeah, Valentine's Day," she said.

Phil looked deeply into her eyes. Stevie kept herself from sighing audibly, but Phil's look made it tempting. Then he leaned toward her, pulling her gently to him.

Gong! Gong! Gong!

Phil sat up straight in surprise. "What's that?" he asked.

"A gong," Stevie answered.

"*What* gong?"

"The Pine Hollow gong," Stevie said, trying to get his attention back to where it had been only a few seconds earlier.

"Why is there a Pine Hollow gong?"

Gong! Gong! Gong!

"It's for emergencies," Stevie explained. She tugged at his hand, but he stood up.

"Like what?" He was clearly concerned. Stevie didn't think he ought to be.

"Like if there's an electrical storm coming or something like that. It means that all the riders, wherever they are, have to get back to the stable as fast as safely possible."

18

"Like us?"

"Oh," Stevie said, realizing that the gong did mean their ride was going to be cut short. "This is annoying," she said. "I hope it doesn't mean that Veronica's mother is trying to reach her to let her know that the chauffeur has to pick her up early."

"But we have to go," Phil said.

Stevie finally relented, knowing he was right. "Yes, we do. If Max rings the gong, everybody's supposed to respond. Even though it isn't about us, he'll be furious if we don't get back. Maybe it's not so bad, though. Once we get back to Pine Hollow, we can take some time to work on the jump course in the ring, okay?"

"Okay," he said, retrieving the horses. "Though, to tell you the truth, I'd rather sit by the creek with you."

"Me too," Stevie told him, knowing she'd have to wait until the Valentine's Day dance to recapture the moment that had been interrupted by the gong. But she *would* recapture it.

They returned to Pine Hollow as quickly as possible. In less than ten minutes the stable was in sight.

That was when Stevie started getting worried, for she could see Carole and Lisa in the field at the back of the stable, perched on the fences. As soon as they spotted Stevie and Phil, they began waving. It wasn't a greeting, it was a hurry-up wave. Stevie nudged Topside and got him to quicken his gait. She felt a little knot tighten in her stomach. Something was wrong, and the closer she got to Pine Hollow, the surer she was something was really wrong and it had to do with her.

"It's Alex!" Lisa called out when she knew Stevie was close enough to hear her.

"What?"

"Alex. He's in the hospital. Your mom said to get over there," Lisa said.

"Mrs. Reg said she'd drive you," Carole told her.

"Here, I'll take Topside," said Lisa.

Alex? What could have happened to him? Stevie wondered, her mind racing. He couldn't have hurt himself in gym or anything, because he was home with a cold. Could he have gotten a burn from the stove? He'd be dumb enough to do that. Or maybe tripped on something? No, he was too surefooted for tripping. Maybe he hurt his finger pushing the remote control for the TV? But the look on her friends' faces told her that this wasn't just a twisted ankle or a sprained finger. This was more serious.

"Your mother said it was his fever," Lisa explained. "He really got sick this afternoon. She even called an ambulance."

"Alex?" She couldn't conceive of it. He'd been okay this morning. He'd had his cold and a headache, but he was okay. In fact, up until last night, when he'd gone to bed without even touching his dinner, Stevie had been sure that he was faking it. Now he'd gone to the hospital in an ambulance? Alex was her brother—her twin brother. He could be a nuisance, he could be a tattle, he could be an idiot, but he was her twin, and she couldn't imagine his being in an ambulance.

"There you are, Stevie," said Mrs. Reg. "Come on, let's go. I've got the car running."

"I'll take care of Topside," said Phil.

Stevie dismounted, handing Phil her reins. She followed Mrs. Reg, barely aware of where she was going or why. All she could see was the image of her brother, her twin, Alex, in the back of an ambulance going to the hospital.

STEVIE SETTLED INTO the seat next to Mrs. Reg. The hospital was a ten-minute drive. That gave her a lot of time to think. Maybe Alex really wasn't so sick. Maybe he'd done that thing with the thermometer that Stevie had tried, holding it up to the lightbulb so it would show a nice high fever. The problem was that lightbulbs could get really hot. Once she'd gotten the mercury all the way to the top of the thing in about six seconds. Maybe that's what it was. Alex wasn't really sick. Just sort of.

"I knew a pair of foals once," Mrs. Reg said. "Not the same mare, just the same age, living at the same stable —a colt and a filly."

Stevie was a little startled. She'd been thinking so

hard about Alex and the lightbulb that she'd almost forgotten Mrs. Reg was there. Mrs. Reg was well known for her stories about horses, and they usually began just the way this one did—with no introduction—and they frequently ended with no conclusion. They were also usually worth listening to. Stevie turned her attention to Mrs. Reg's tale.

"This pair, when they weren't with their mares, were always together. They'd been born just hours apart in adjoining stalls. They took their first walks outside together, they were halter trained the same day. They were taught to be on leads at the same time. First the trainer would take one, then the other. They were just always together, and they were quick learners. It seemed like when one of them learned something, both of them learned it—like they could teach each other. Then, when they were about two, the trainer separated them and sold them. The colt went to a riding school; the filly to a private owner.

"The colt did pretty well. The trainer there worked with him and found him to be a good learner. By the time he was three, the trainer was riding him. By the time he was five, the students were on him. He was spirited but okay, at least for the really good students, giving them just enough trouble that they learned while they rode him. He was a useful horse except for the fact that he always refused to jump."

Mrs. Reg smiled as if remembering. That made Stevie think that the riding school was probably Pine Hollow. Max didn't often have the time to train a school horse from the start, but he always said the best way to be sure a horse was well trained was to do it yourself.

"What was the colt's name?" Stevie asked, hoping she knew the horse.

"Name? I don't know," said Mrs. Reg. Stevie suspected she did know. She just thought that would be a distraction to the rest of her story. "He was a grade horse, mind you. Nothing special in his bloodlines, but there was a lot special in his heart. Just sometimes it was hard to tell because he was so ornery and wouldn't jump."

"What about the filly?"

Mrs. Reg gave her a look. She didn't like to have questions during her stories. She liked to tell them at her own pace.

"The filly went to a private barn belonging to a family of riders. They took very good care of her and worked with her every single day. Their daughter wanted to be a professional rider and thought the filly would be a test of her training skills."

Mrs. Reg paused, looking out across the boulevard to

see if she could make a left turn. When the traffic cleared, she pulled out, turned left, and resumed her story.

"Where was I?"

"The filly being a test of the girl's training skills. Was she?"

"Oh, yes, she was," Mrs. Reg said. "The girl had all the patience in the world. She worked for a couple of hours every day, but the horse never got the idea. She was always an upstart. She wouldn't stand still to have her bridle put on. She'd nip and kick and buck. It was two years before the girl thought she'd try to get into the saddle, and another two years before she wanted to try it a second time. That filly was simply a handful. By that time the girl was ready to give up. Her father bought her another horse to work with, and they sold the filly—now a full-grown, apparently untrainable mare."

"A breeder?"

"Yes, a breeder bought her. She was a beauty, no doubt about that, but she was no good as a saddle horse, and though, like the colt, she was a grade horse, she'd still do for breeding—that is, if the stallion had a willing disposition, since she certainly didn't."

Stevie knew that breeders tried to match up horses with complementary strong qualities so that the offspring could inherit the good qualities of their parents. A mare with a sweet disposition but not much speed might be bred with a stallion who could move fast but had a rotten disposition, in the hopes that the offspring would be a speedy, good-natured horse. Of course that sometimes resulted in a grumpy slowpoke, but breeders hoped for the best.

"It turned out she wasn't much of a mother, either. She had a few foals and they were all right, but they weren't anything very special, so the breeder decided to sell her. He was somewhat less than totally honest. He sold the mare, along with a few other horses, to a riding school, without saying anything about how unsuitable the mare was for riding at all, much less for young riders."

"Was this the same riding school?" Stevie asked curiously.

Mrs. Reg ignored the question.

"Well, the owner of the riding school put one rider on the mare, saw how impossible she was, and decided to sell her the next day."

It wasn't the same riding school, Stevie concluded.

"It was the same riding school that the colt had been sold to," said Mrs. Reg.

Stevie was confused but decided not to ask any more

26

questions. Mrs. Reg was clearly going to tell her story the way she wanted to tell it.

"Well, the riding instructor took that mare to a trainer nearby, a trainer he often bought horses from and sold them to as well. This stable owner thought the trainer might use the ornery mare for breeding—though of course he didn't know that the mare wasn't much better at that than she was at being a school horse. The nearby trainer was the same man from whom the instructor had bought the colt. He'd sold him back that colt, too, because although he was a pretty good horse, he was never gentle enough for the children and new riders who rode at the stable, and the more experienced riders always expected to jump.

"People who saw the mare arrive still tell the story, you know."

"What story?"

"About the mare arriving," said Mrs. Reg.

"Arriving?"

"Back at the trainer's farm. Where she'd started from." There was a slight tone of annoyance in Mrs. Reg's voice, as if Stevie should have figured this all out by now.

"The minute they opened the rear of the trailer," Mrs. Reg went on, "the mare became totally docile—unlike anything anyone had ever seen from her. She looked around and there was the colt, now a full-gown gelded horse, standing in a paddock. He spotted her at the same time. The mare, who'd been feisty as all get-out getting on the van, simply walked off the thing. It was a funny deal, because a whole bunch of people were standing around with extra leads, blindfolds, carrots, what-have-you, and she did it all by herself. Then, without so much as a thank you, she trotted right over to the fence of the paddock where the gelding was watching. He took one look at her and did the one thing he'd never done before. He jumped. He just plain backed up to give himself space, galloped to the fence, and jumped, clearing it with six inches to spare. Nobody had ever been able to get him to jump at all before.

"The trainer and all his helpers, the stable hands, the driver, were all standing trying to clip lead ropes onto the gelding or tug at the mare's lead, but it was the trainer who realized what was going on.

" 'Stand back,' he said. And everybody did. There wasn't any need to do anything else anyway. See, the two horses stood face-to-face and sniffed at one another, nodding their heads up in the air, just like they were saying 'Yes!' Then they nuzzled one another and rubbed their cheeks against each other."

"True love," Stevie said.

"Maybe," said Mrs. Reg. "But whatever it was, it worked. Right there in front of a whole crowd of people, two horses completely changed their personalities. The gelding who had been difficult suddenly became cooperative and became a great jumper. The mare who had been impossible turned docile. They each seemed to remember everything everybody had ever tried to teach them, and they really didn't need any training. Within a few weeks the trainer sent the pair back to the stable, where they were both wonderful riding horses for generations of students."

Stevie thought about that for a few minutes. Mrs. Reg's stories usually required some thinking. Sometimes they seemed to be one thing but were really another. Usually they were actually two things at once. Stevie thought there might be something missing from this one.

"What happened if they ever got separated again?" Stevie asked. "Like one horse going on a trail ride and the other working in class or on the jump course."

"I told you," Mrs. Reg said. "They were good horses. No problems."

Clearly, that was all that Mrs. Reg was going to say. Stevie would have to do the figuring on her own.

"Here we are," said Mrs. Reg, turning into the hospital. She pulled round to the emergency-room entrance.

It occurred to Stevie then that perhaps Mrs. Reg had just rustled this story up out of her store of tales to keep Stevie's mind off the fact that something might be really wrong. It had worked, but all the good the tale had done vanished the second Stevie saw her mother standing by the emergency-room door, waiting for her. Her mother's face was pale and drawn. Something was very wrong.

CAROLE AND LISA looked around the food-storage barn. Carole had her hands on her hips. Lisa chewed thoughtfully on her tongue. It was a way she had of thinking logically. It wasn't easy to think logically right then, because both she and Carole were concerned about Stevie's brother. Worry wasn't going to do them any good, though, so they were trying to think about the dance and how they might decorate for it.

Pine Hollow stored all its grains and hay in an outbuilding away from the stable where the horses resided. Grains and hay were highly flammable and subject to spontaneous combustion. Max took all the proper precautions to be sure that the materials didn't start a fire, but if it should happen, he particularly wanted to be sure that all he lost would be the grains, hay, and the building that contained them—not the horses.

"I think Max is getting a little low on hay," Carole observed. "That's bad news for the horses."

"Ah, but it's good news for us," said Lisa. "You're so tuned in to the horses' needs that you forgot we're going to have to make room for a dance in here. We can hardly make squares of eight if the whole place is filled with bales of hay. Come on, let's see if we can move enough of them to make a dance floor."

The bales of hay weighed about fifty pounds each. They were too heavy for either Carole or Lisa to lift by herself, but if each took hold of an end, they could move them around.

"You know, if we stack them right," said Lisa, "like three high at the back, two high in front of that, and then just one, I bet we could make something like a gallery—a place where people can sit."

"Great idea," Carole said, seeing what Lisa had in mind. "If only we had a forklift to save us from lugging these things around by hand."

"Ahem," came a voice from the door. The girls turned and saw Phil standing there. "Did someone call my name?"

"Huh?" Carole said.

"Forklift," he explained. "I've been working with weights to build my strength for the wrestling team, and I keep looking for an opportunity to show off the incredible force of my biceps, triceps, and lats. I'm like a knight in shining muscles looking for a damsel or two in distress. Have I come to the right place?"

Carole and Lisa never had any trouble understanding what it was that Stevie saw in Phil. They thought he was funny and nice, too, and they were glad he was their friend as well.

"Absolutely," Carole said. "Come show off for us. Play your cards right and we might even help you."

"Okay, tell me what you've got in mind," Phil said.

The girls explained their idea about creating a gallery, and Phil helped them improve on the plan—explaining how they could strengthen the gallery and make it more secure by putting the bales at angles to one another. Then they got to work.

The three of them cleared a space that would be large enough for a dance floor, and then they began stacking the bales. Lisa's idea, improved upon by Phil and executed by all three of them, turned out to be a very good one. The graduated stacks of hay bales gave the barn a feeling that Lisa described as "very barny." Since it was a barn, that seemed appropriate to Carole and Phil. They completed the stacks, omitting the number of bales that they figured the stable would use by the time of the dance, and felt that they'd done a good job.

"Okay, now, time for crepe paper," Lisa said.

Phil had a number of ideas on how to decorate with crepe paper, and they discussed that. They also discussed where the band should stand, how the PA system could be used, how much food they would need, where it would be put, how many dancers would probably come, how they could find ways to get the kids to dance, mixing with one another so that everybody would have a chance to dance. They talked about almost every imaginable topic having to do with the dance and with Pine Hollow and with horses. They just didn't talk about Alex.

They all knew how much Stevie always complained about her brothers, how she would pick fights with them and play tricks on them. She was a genius at revenge if one of them played a trick on her or tried to sabotage her friendship with Phil. She claimed to wish on a daily basis that she were an only child. They also knew how she would stand up for Michael, Chad, and Alex if anybody else ever dared to criticize any one of them. It was *her* right to be angry at her brothers; nobody else could have that privilege. She loved them too much to let any other person insult them.

"Look, we've got plenty of dancing room now," said

Lisa. She was standing on top of the highest bale of hay, admiring all they'd accomplished.

"Want to try out the dance floor?" Phil asked. He offered his hand to help her down. She took it and stepped down regally, one bale at a time.

"They're nice and steady," she said. "Thanks to you."

"You're welcome," he said. Then, when Lisa reached the stable floor, Phil turned to Carole. "Maestro, some music, please."

Carole obliged. She puckered her lips and began whistling "Turkey in the Straw."

Phil put his right hand on Lisa's waist, took her right hand with his left, and began doing a two-step. They shuffled the full length of the floor, turning and bouncing with every step.

Carole thought they looked wonderful, enjoying themselves on the dance floor. It made her think how much she was looking forward to doing the same thing with her special friend, Cam. Cam was a rider she'd met through a computer bulletin board. They'd been sending notes back and forth furiously, each trying to prove he or she knew more about horses than the other. Then when they'd met in person, they'd realized it didn't matter who knew more. The important thing was they both liked horses—and each other. Carole got to see Cam a little less frequently than Stevie saw Phil, but each time was very special. This Valentine's Day dance would be no exception to that, she was sure.

"Next!" Phil called out, delivering Lisa to the "band-stand."

"I can't whistle like Carole, you know," Lisa said. "I'm all out of breath."

"Just do what you can," Phil suggested.

Lisa looked around for inspiration. There was a small toolbox that they'd borrowed from Max—just in case. She opened it and found a couple of screwdrivers. Then she turned her attention to the barrels of mixed grain in an alcove that had once served as a goat pen. Just what she needed. Tentatively, she tapped on the lids of the barrels. Each was filled with a different quantity of grain, so they made slightly different tones, quite like bottles filled with different amounts of liquids. There wasn't much variety, but there was enough. Much to Carole and Phil's amazement, she began pounding out a reggae beat—very un-barn-dance-like, but lots of fun. Carole and Phil got right into the mood and started dancing to Lisa's music.

They were on the second verse of Lisa's improvised song when the barn door opened, filling the room with cool winter light. Mrs. Reg came in. Her face was grim.

The music and dancing stopped immediately.

"What is it?" Lisa asked. "What's wrong with Alex?"

"They're doing tests," she said. "They don't know for sure, but . . ."

"He just had a cold," said Phil. "How bad could that be?"

"It could be meningitis," said Mrs. Reg. "That's what they think, and that's what they're testing for."

"Meningitis? How could he get that?" asked Carole.

"There's really no way of telling how he got it," said Mrs. Reg.

"Then how do they know he *does* have it?" Carole asked.

"All the symptoms," Mrs. Reg said. "He started out with flu symptoms, then they got a lot worse, then he had a bad headache and a high fever. Then his neck got stiff. Finally, he got a rash. Those are all pretty strong indicators that this is meningitis."

"What do they do about it?" Lisa asked.

"How's Stevie?" asked Phil.

"Could she get it?" Carole asked.

Mrs. Reg sat down on one of the bales of hay. She seemed to need to rest, and it was clear she was going to do the best job she could to give them information. She took a deep breath and began. "You have a lot of questions, and I have some of the answers because I knew you'd want to know, so I talked to the doctor. Then I called my own doctor to be sure I understood. The most important thing that he said to me was that our hospital is well equipped to take care of Alex. He'll get the best possible treatment there. Now, here goes. First of all, Stevie's fine, though unusually quiet—"

"She gets that way sometimes," Phil said. He didn't mean to be funny, but since Stevie was almost always talking or laughing, what he'd said *was* funny, and her friends couldn't help laughing a little bit. It felt good.

Mrs. Reg smiled. "Not often, though," she said. "Anyway, the doctor explained to me that this kind of meningitis is usually given to one person from another, about the same way cold germs are passed around. Because a person is so sick with meningitis when they're most contagious, they're not likely to be around other people, so it's not easily passed around except to people who are near you. What that means is that Stevie, her parents, and her other brothers may have been exposed, and the doctors will give them a preventive vaccine. Based on what I've heard from Stevie, she tries to stay away from her brothers, anyway, so I think she's safe."

"That's just talk," Phil said. "She really loves them a lot."

"I know she does," Mrs. Reg said. "I was trying to be funny. The bottom line, though, is that the vaccine will protect her. She'll be fine."

"And Alex?"

Mrs. Reg shrugged. She really didn't know. She told them that the doctors didn't, either. "Meningitis is a very serious disease. They've taken a sample of the infected fluids, and they'll test them to see exactly what kind of infection they're dealing with."

"They don't know?" Phil asked.

"Not really," said Mrs. Reg. "See, meningitis simply means there's an inflammation of the meninges—that's the membrane that surrounds and protects the brain. A lot of different things can inflame it. With the symptoms that Alex has, they can be pretty sure it's bacterial, which means it should respond to an antibiotic. They started giving him a range of antibiotics before they did almost anything else to him. They'll test the fluid to see if the specific bacterium responds to one of the antibiotics better than another. If it does, they'll use that one. In the meantime it's sort of a shotgun approach. They're sure to be doing some good and no harm that way."

"What happens next?" Lisa asked.

"Waiting. A lot of waiting. Alex is unconscious now."

Lisa could feel her stomach tighten with fear. "He's in a coma?"

"I guess that's what it is," said Mrs. Reg. "The doctor said that wasn't unusual."

"How long will that be?"

"That was a question I asked my own doctor. He said it could last a couple of hours or a couple of weeks. There's no way to tell, and there's no way to predict how he'll be when he comes out of the coma."

"He'll get better then, won't he?" Lisa asked. She needed the reassurance.

"We can hope," Mrs. Reg said. "In fact, we should hope. A lot. In the meantime we should do everything we can to help Stevie. She's upset—as you can imagine."

Lisa could imagine. She looked at Carole and Phil. The three of them were Stevie's best friends—the other members of The Saddle Club. Helping out a friend sometimes meant just being there. Lisa thought this was probably one of those times. If that was what Stevie needed, all three of them would be there for her as long as she needed it.

Mrs. Reg stood up then and said something about having to get to some desk work.

When the door closed behind her, Lisa realized that she was still holding on to the two screwdrivers that so recently had been making cheerful music on the drums of grains. She looked for a place to put them down, embarrassed by the joyful sound they'd made. Carole took them from her and put them back into the toolbox. When she turned back to Lisa and Phil, they could see that she had tears in her eyes, finally expressing what they'd been feeling, too.

Phil reached out his arms to the girls. He needed their comfort, and they needed his as well as one another's. Lisa and Carole came to him, hugging tightly, tears of sadness and fear rolling unbidden down their cheeks. They had one another, and Stevie had them. It seemed like a meager defense against a brutal illness.

Stevie's mind was so full that she didn't even feel the needle when the doctor gave her the vaccine to protect her against getting meningitis. All she could think of was her brother, lying on the hospital bed on the other side of the glass wall. He wasn't moving. He wasn't crying or complaining. He wasn't even being a nuisance. He was just lying there.

Stevie stood up from the chair and looked again, hoping that he might have moved a little bit, but he hadn't. He was completely still, breathing evenly, almost as if he were asleep.

Asleep. That's what she told herself. Alex was having a deep, restful, healing sleep. He'd awake from it in the morning, sit up in the hospital bed, wonder how he'd gotten there, and then he'd start being a pain in the neck to Stevie again. That's what she wanted. She wanted Alex to be himself. Even though he could be a nuisance, a tattle, a bully, and everything else in the book, that was the way she wanted him.

The neurologist's words still rang in her ears, an echoing reminder of how sick Alex was. Meningitis. Coma. Antibiotics. Serious. Possible permanent damage. Hearing loss. Headache. Neck ache.

Alex had said something about his neck aching last night. Stevie hadn't paid any attention to it, though. There hadn't seemed to be anything unusual about it. She always thought of her brothers as a pain in the neck.

She should have known.

She'd taken health classes. She'd seen movies. Stiffness and pain in the neck could be serious. Could be meningitis. She should have worried last night. She should have told their mother. Maybe. Just maybe.

Stevie shook her head. She peered at her brother. Then she remembered yesterday afternoon.

Alex had been sick. He'd wanted something—her horse, her precious chocolate horse—and she hadn't let him have it. She'd screamed at him. That was the last time she'd spoken to him.

The last time. The thought spun in her head.

"Stevie?" It was her father. He stood behind her and gave her a hug from behind. They both looked through the glass at Alex, who didn't move. Plastic sacks of liquids hung upside down, dripping into tubes that went into a needle in his arm. They didn't look like much—clear liquids, not much different from water. The tubes tangled, the bags dripped. Alex lay still.

"They're doing everything they can," her father said.

"We should have brought him sooner," said Stevie.

"We didn't know sooner," her father said.

But Stevie thought she should have known, and she knew now that she never should have thought Alex had been faking. There had been so many signs. How could she have missed them?

These thoughts filled her mind, going nowhere, accomplishing nothing while she watched her brother.

"We're going home now for a little while," Mrs. Lake said. "We'll have some dinner and then we'll come back. The doctor said he's okay for now. Nothing will happen for a while. He's stable. That's what the doctor said."

Stevie couldn't leave Alex. He was her twin—her other half. She couldn't eat anything, anyway, so what difference would it make if she went home or not?

"I want to stay," she said.

Mrs. Lake didn't protest. She understood. This brother and sister had shared everything since before they'd been born. Although they fought like a lot of brothers and sisters, there had always been a special bond. Everyone in the family knew it and respected it. Now that Alex was sick, Mrs. Lake wasn't surprised Stevie wanted to stay near him. Stevie sometimes had funny ways of showing her love for Alex, but it was always there.

"We'll bring you back something to eat," Mrs. Lake said.

"Okay."

Chad and Michael stood by their mother. They understood, too.

Mr. and Mrs. Lake and the boys left. Stevie was alone with her thoughts and her inert brother. Around her, visitors shuffled down the hall, nurses bustled around their station and in and out of the rooms, and doctors strode by, responding to the calls of the PA system that clicked on and off regularly. Stevie saw and heard none of this.

She sank down onto the sofa and lay back, closing her eyes.

Again and again she could see Alex in her room,

standing by the window, holding the chocolate horse.
She could almost touch the memory of her own anger,
and she was deeply ashamed of it. Her brother was sick,
very sick, and she'd missed the chance to do something
for him.

Alex had done so much for her. Stevie recalled a
time when the two of them were about six and they'd
decided to climb a tree their mother had told them to
stay away from. Stevie had fallen out of the tree and
scraped her knee. Alex took care of her. He'd washed
the cut and bandaged it and even loaned her some of
his jeans so she could keep wearing long pants until it
healed. He'd never told anybody about it, either.

Once their older cousin from Toronto had come for a
visit and had teased Stevie about being a tomboy with a
tomboy's name. Alex had punched him—just for her.
And then there was the time Alex had invited a boy in
their class over to play Nintendo because Stevie
thought he was cute, even though Alex didn't like him
at all. When Stevie had changed her mind about the
boy because he'd cheated at cards, Alex hadn't even
teased her about it very much.

Stevie remembered, too, hundreds of times when
she'd forgotten her schoolbooks and Alex had shared,
saving her from the wrath of dozens of teachers.

He'd done so many things for her and in return, what had she done for him? Stevie couldn't think of a thing. Not one thing.

She wanted to make a difference to him. If she could love him enough, be the sister he'd always hoped he'd had, do things the right way instead of the funny or clever way. Maybe that would be enough. Maybe Alex would get better.

Stevie felt a new resolve coming to her. First of all, she wasn't going to leave Alex—not for a minute if she didn't have to. Sure, her parents would make her go to school, and she'd have to do some other things, but until Alex was better, she was going to spend every spare minute at the hospital. She'd give up riding, her friends, everything fun until he was well. She cared about Alex, and that was one way to show him. If she had strength and courage, she could share it with him. Those weren't the same as antibiotics, but it was the best she could do, and she wanted to do it for Alex.

Next, she wasn't going to be a nuisance anymore— not to anybody. She'd get her homework done; she'd stop getting C's and only get A's; she'd stop making wisecracks; no more practical jokes; no more rude retorts; no more thoughtless, careless, heartless Stevie. She had a new and wonderful person inside her, and that person was going to be a loving, kind, supportive sister to her beloved twin brother. Alex would get better. He'd have to get better. And when he did that, he'd find that he had a better sister, too, and she would never, ever again have a fight with him.

As soon as the doctor said it was okay for her to be in Alex's room, she'd be right by his bedside. She'd wipe his forehead with a cool cloth. She'd read to him. She'd make him his favorite marshmallow crunchies—the ones she never let him have any of when she made a batch with Lisa and Carole. Well, those days were gone. Alex was going to be her number-one concern from now on.

Stevie sat upright. She had work to do—homework. She remembered that her English assignment for tomorrow was to write a brief essay about metaphors. She couldn't do her math assignment or study for her history test without the textbooks, but she could write the essay as long as she had some paper.

She fished in her pocket for some change and called home. Chad answered. She told him Alex was the same and asked if he would bring her school backpack to the hospital when he came after dinner. He agreed and promised they'd bring her a sandwich, too.

"Don't bother. I really can't eat," she said. "I just need to work a little bit, though."

Chad agreed, though he seemed a little confused, and Stevie wasn't surprised. Usually, Stevie found the weakest possible excuses not to do her homework. Now that she actually had a real excuse, one that was a lot stronger than a recent one she'd used about having an ingrown toenail, she was choosing to work on her assignments.

As soon as she hung up with Chad, Stevie went to the nurses' station and asked if anybody had a pad of paper and a pencil she could borrow to do her homework. One of the nurses, a young woman whose name tag identified her as Beverly Earl, provided a yellow pad and a ballpoint pen.

"Will this do?" she asked. "There are only about three sheets left on the pad. I hope that's enough."

"Sure," said Stevie. "I have to write an essay on everything I know about metaphors. Three sheets should do it."

The nurse smiled at her. "A scratch pad would do it for me on that subject," she joked.

Stevie smiled at her in recognition of a sort of common bond. That's exactly what she might have said, too, before. Now she was sure she could come up with more than a scratch pad's worth.

She returned to the bench outside Alex's room,

peered in, assuring herself that he was still sleeping restfully, and sat down with determination.

She looked at the pad. She looked at the pen. This essay wasn't going to write itself. She was going to have to do the work. She could do it.

Metaphors are the heart of all great literature, she began.

AT THE FIRST sound of her alarm, Stevie was up and out of bed in the morning. She showered, dressed, packed up her books neatly, made her bed, and was downstairs even before her mother. She poured herself a bowl of cereal, added milk—no sugar—ate it, drank a glass of orange juice, rinsed the bowl, spoon, and glass, put them in the dishwasher, and left the house for school. She glanced at her watch. In earlier times she would have been giving the snooze button on her clock radio a third slap at this hour, rather than leaving the house. She smiled to herself, feeling good about what she was doing. It was working already. She *was* a better person.

The walk to school was a short one, only about fifteen minutes, but this morning it took longer because she ran into so many friends of hers and Alex's. Everybody wanted to know how he was.

"He's very sick," she said. "He's got meningitis, but the doctors are doing everything they can for him, and he's going to get better. I just know it."

A lot of the kids didn't know much about meningitis, and Stevie was glad to tell them everything she knew. That included what the neurologist had said as well as what she'd looked up in the encyclopedia the night before. She explained about the difference between bacterial versus viral meningitis and how antibiotics were used to combat it and how they were testing to find exactly the right one, but in the meantime they were using everything. When she got to school, it seemed that the whole rest of her class was there, wanting information as well. Stevie stood on the steps of Fenton Hall, explaining everything all over again. The thing they mostly wanted to know was about Alex, though. How *was* he?

"He's been sleeping," Stevie said. "I guess it's a coma. That's what the doctor said. I think it's like a deep sleep so that his body can work on fighting the infection without having to worry about anything else, like walking, sitting, or talking. That's what I think, anyway."

She glanced at her watch. It was just fifteen minutes

52

until the first bell rang, and there was so much to do. She had to go to her locker and then get to her homeroom. This was an activity that usually took her two minutes because that was as much time as she usually allowed for it. This morning, however, the new Stevie had other chores. She had some pencils to sharpen, too. "Got to get inside now," she said. Her friends stepped aside and let her pass.

Inside, the teachers had all the same concerns that Stevie's friends had. Even Miss Fenton, the headmistress, came to Stevie for information. Stevie was used to talking to Miss Fenton and explaining things to her, but those things were usually unexplainable—like how a wad of bubble gum got onto a teacher's chair, or why Veronica diAngelo's sneakers had turned green overnight. This time Miss Fenton was very gentle and caring and sympathetic.

"These are difficult times, Stevie," she said. "You may find your attention wandering more than usual. If you need extra help, just let me or your teachers know. We're here to help you, and we'll be here to help Alex —when he gets better."

Stevie thanked her. "I don't think you'll have to help me, though," she said. "I'll be doing fine, I'm sure, and as soon as Alex is a little better, I can tutor him and help him to catch up on all the subjects, except maybe Spanish because he takes that and I take French."

"That would be wonderful," Miss Fenton said. "But sometimes things don't work out exactly the way we expect them to, and you may find that sometimes schoolwork seems less important than other things. We understand this, Stevie. Just let us know."

"Thanks, but it won't be necessary," Stevie assured her again. Then she had to dash off to her homeroom. Now she had only eight minutes to sharpen those pencils. Miss Fenton had meant well, but she hadn't understood. That was okay. Like everyone else, she would see the change in Stevie eventually. For now it was enough for Stevie to know about it.

It turned out that Stevie didn't have any time at all to sharpen her pencils, because the minute she got to her classroom, Miss Fenton announced a schoolwide assembly. All students, faculty, and any parents who were at the school that morning were invited to come immediately.

As they entered the assembly hall, Stevie felt a lot of eyes on her. The looks were of concern, sympathy, and wonder. She realized that by now just about everyone knew that Alex was in the hospital and they were all curious. Some had other reactions, too.

It turned out that the assembly had to do with Alex.

Miss Fenton told everybody—as if they didn't already know—about his meningitis. Then she explained what she knew about the disease. She also said that to the best of their knowledge nobody else at the school was infected, and it seemed very unlikely that they would be. It was a disease that was spread only by close contact, and since Alex had been out of school for a couple of days already, a doctor had assured her that he almost certainly wouldn't have infected anyone at school. Then she explained that Alex's family had been given vaccinations, so they wouldn't infect anybody, either. What she was getting at was that school was going to continue as usual, and nobody should stay home just because Alex was sick.

Stevie looked straight forward, gazing firmly at Miss Fenton. She was very aware of the fact that almost everybody in the assembly hall was looking at her, and she could imagine what was going on in their minds. Some of them were feeling pity, most of the rest were wondering if she was carrying any germs they should be worried about.

Stevie didn't care what they were thinking. All she knew was that her brother was ill and she had a job to do to see that he got better.

Miss Fenton dismissed the assembly. The bell rang. It was time for math class.

Miss Snyder always began the class by having the students correct one another's homework papers.

"Okay, everybody swap papers," she said. She did allow the students to choose which other student got to look at the work they'd done, which had often spared Stevie the humiliation of having somebody she didn't like sneer at her mistakes. Stevie was reaching for her bag with her assignment in it when Miss Snyder suggested that she just look on with somebody else.

"But I've got the assignment here," she said, producing it.

"You do?" The teacher was clearly surprised. Stevie knew she was recalling dozens of weak excuses she'd heard from Stevie, and that she'd just assumed Stevie wouldn't have gotten her homework done in the face of a real problem.

"Sure," she said. "I had a lot of time to work at the hospital yesterday. It was pretty quiet, so I just did my work."

"Well, uh, good," Miss Snyder said. "Very good." She smiled, her surprise turning to pleasure.

That made Stevie feel good. Finally somebody was appreciating her new way of living her life. That must mean that it was working. She was sure Alex must feel her own happiness at the new and improved Stevie.

It turned out that she *was* a new and improved

Stevie, because she got eighteen of the twenty problems correct. Miss Snyder was even more pleased by that than she was by the fact that Stevie had done them.

"*Very* good," she said to Stevie as the members of the class filed out. "I knew you could do it."

"I have to work extra hard these days," Stevie replied. "See, I'm going to have to help Alex catch up when he gets better."

"Yes," said Miss Snyder. "I understand."

Some of Stevie's other teachers didn't understand as well as Miss Snyder did. They weren't used to the new Stevie, and a few of them even indicated that they didn't *believe* the new Stevie—as if this were just another one of her practical jokes. They'll see, eventually, Stevie told herself, especially when her history teacher graded her test. She was pretty sure she had aced it.

As soon as the last class was over, Stevie checked to make sure she knew what all her assignments were, and then she selected the books she'd need, made sure she had paper and sharp pencils, straightened out her locker, and left for the hospital.

Chad and Michael got out of school at the same time, but they were going home. Stevie didn't want to waste any time at home when Alex needed her by his bedside.

She got a lift from a parent who lived near the hospital. She was there by three-thirty—the hour she usually arrived at Pine Hollow.

Alex was still sleeping. Beverly, the nurse, told Stevie that he seemed to be doing well.

"His fever is down a little," Beverly said.

"But he's still unconscious." Stevie had been hoping that he'd be more improved by now.

"There is no way to predict how long he'll be unconscious," Beverly reminded Stevie. "You have to look for other signs. The fever dropping is a good sign. It means the antibiotics are working."

"Oh."

When Stevie was satisfied that Alex was comfortable and everything needed had been done for him, she made a quick call to Pine Hollow. She knew her friends would be worried about Alex and wondering about her. Mrs. Reg answered the phone. Stevie told her what was happening and explained that she wouldn't be riding for a while. Mrs. Reg seemed to understand. She told Stevie that Lisa and Carole were just in the paddock and offered to call them to the phone. Stevie said no, she didn't have time for that now. Mrs. Reg sounded surprised at that, but Stevie didn't offer any explanation. Stevie said a hurried good-bye and then settled down on the bench she'd claimed as her own the night before and began her assignments.

In spite of all the activity around her, Stevie found it very easy to concentrate on her work. She was determined that the only thing that would distract her would be Alex, so she allowed herself to stand up and look through the glass at her resting brother every five minutes—or after every math problem when she was doing math.

Once she thought that Alex had changed positions. She wasn't absolutely certain, but he seemed to be comfortable. That was what was important.

At about five-thirty her mother arrived. She'd been there earlier and she was coming back, just to check on Alex and to bring Stevie home.

"He's better, I think," Stevie said to her mother. "Beverly told me that his temperature is down. That's a good sign."

Her mother nodded. "Yes, it is," she said. "Very good." Her mother put her arm around Stevie's shoulder, and the two of them looked through the glass at Alex.

"It's time to go home," Mrs. Lake said. "Dinner. Dad's cooking. He wanted to make a meat loaf."

"I'm staying here," Stevie said. "You can bring me something later." Much as she wanted to be with Alex, she wasn't completely willing to miss her father's meat loaf.

"No, I want you to come home," said Mrs. Lake. "We should all have dinner together tonight."

Stevie began to protest. She really felt her place was with Alex, but she remembered that part of her promise to herself about self-improvement was that she wasn't going to be a fussy nuisance anymore. If her mother wanted her home, then she would go home. She packed up her books neatly, and the two of them left together.

Stevie found that Michael had set the table. Usually he hated setting the table and did anything he could to get out of it. Stevie wasn't at all surprised. Michael must be feeling a little bit the way she was. Chad, on the other hand, was up in his room, reading *The Yearling*. It had been his favorite book when he was ten.

Stevie put the glasses on the table and poured milk. When Mr. Lake pronounced dinner ready, everybody came to the table.

"How's Alex?" Chad asked Stevie. She told him she thought he was a little better because his fever was down and he'd moved some.

"Wow, Dad's meat loaf!" Michael said enthusiastically.

Michael had already known what was for dinner. It seemed odd that he would express surprise at this point. But Stevie understood. She found, in fact, that she understood a lot of things. She understood that every

60

member of her family was worrying about Alex in his or her own way. Dad was cooking; Michael was pitching in; Chad was hanging out by himself; and Stevie was staying by Alex's bedside. Stevie wasn't sure how her mother was coping until she saw the gigantic pile of freshly ironed sheets. Her mother *never* ironed sheets. They always used them just the way they came out of the laundry.

Stevie understood, too, that when Alex got better, everybody would probably revert to their old selves—everybody, that was, except Stevie. She was a better person, and she was determined to stay that way.

The family ate in silence, nobody knowing what to say, except for the frequent compliments to Mr. Lake for his meat loaf.

"I never make it the same way twice," he said. That's what he always said.

"I'll do the dishes," Stevie volunteered when she'd taken her last bite.

"No, I will," said Michael.

"Why don't you all do them together?" Mrs. Lake suggested, looking at the three children.

"No way!" said Chad. "If those two want to do the dishes, they can. Count me out. I've got a lot of work to do, anyway." He stood up from the table and dashed upstairs. Nobody said anything.

Quietly, Stevie and Michael did the dishes. They didn't splash each other. They didn't snap dish towels at each other. Neither complained about having to do the job. Nothing was the way it usually was.

When morning came, Stevie reminded her mother that she'd be going straight to the hospital after school again.

"It's not a good idea, Stevie," Mrs. Lake said, putting the finishing touches on one more well-ironed sheet.

"I have to, Mom," Stevie said, protesting.

"Not today," said her mother. "The doctor has scheduled a test for this afternoon. Alex won't be in his room most of the time. I think you should go be with your friends. . . ."

Her friends? Stevie had almost forgotten about them, and that surprised her.

"You should go to Pine Hollow," her mother continued. "Take a trail ride or work on the decorations for the dance."

Stevie hadn't been thinking about the dance. It was going to be a week from tomorrow. That was a long time away. A lot could happen in a week, but one of the things that almost certainly wouldn't happen was Stevie's going to the dance. There was no way she could romp around a barn while Alex was ill.

"Mom, I don't think—"

"You can go to the hospital after dinner if you want," Mrs. Lake said firmly. "You shouldn't be there this afternoon. Go. Be with Carole and Lisa. I bet they miss you a lot."

Stevie hesitated. If her mother wanted her to go to Pine Hollow, then she should go to Pine Hollow. She wouldn't have any fun there, because she'd be thinking about Alex all the time—but she'd go. That would ease her mother's mind, and her mother's mind could probably use some easing about now.

"Sure, Mom. I'll go to Pine Hollow. Want me to make dinner tonight when I'm done?"

It may have been recollections of previous meals that Stevie had cooked, or it might have been the fact that Mrs. Lake actually already had something planned, but she assured Stevie that she'd take care of dinner.

Stevie picked up her book bag with all her fully completed homework and left the house just in time to get to school fifteen minutes early again.

7

"I HAVEN'T SEEN her or talked to her, have you?"

Carole cradled the phone under her chin and settled more deeply into her father's recliner. She and Lisa were talking about Stevie, and that meant it was going to be a serious conversation.

"Not once—at least not since the time she showed up last week at Pine Hollow for half an hour because her mother had said she had to get out of the hospital."

Lisa sighed. "It's just not like Stevie," she said.

"Well, it's not like Stevie to have a very sick brother, either," said Carole.

"Even so, she's not herself. Stevie's always been a

people person. If anything goes wrong, she always needs to talk about it."

"With us, mostly," Carole said, completing Lisa's thought. "Especially when she needs us to help her solve the problem—"

"Which she usually brings on herself."

"Which isn't the case here," said Carole.

"But I sure wish it were."

"What?"

"I wish this were one of those things that Stevie, like, gets into. You know, the way she's always getting into trouble just when she thinks she's getting out of it, and then when everything looks the very worst, she comes to us and rooks us into helping her actually get out of it. She comes up with some crazy scheme that's totally impossible, and the next thing you know, the problem's solved."

"Like the elephant?" Carole said, recalling one of Stevie's most outrageous schemes. She'd talked a circus owner into letting his elephant cover the scent of a phony fox trail that had been laid by her brother and Veronica diAngelo in order to ruin a hunt.

"Yeah," agreed Lisa. "Just like the elephant. Anyway, if this were simple enough that a mere elephant could solve the problem, then there would hardly be any problem at all."

"But it's not," Carole reminded her.

"I think we should talk to her," said Lisa.

"What if we're bothering her when we call?"

"We're her best friends. How could we be a bother?"

That was a question worth thinking about. As Carole knew, when there was illness in the house, there were some times when a phone call could be a bother, but most of the time they weren't a bother—except when people were just being nosy, and that wasn't what she and Lisa had in mind at all. Stevie was their friend. She might not know that she needed to have her friends around, but she almost certainly did need them and if she had to be reminded of that, well, that was what The Saddle Club was about, anyway. The members had to be willing to pitch in and help one another out—even when the person who needed help didn't know it. That seemed to describe Stevie perfectly right then and there.

"Yes, let's call," said Carole. "Hang on a second, I can make a three-way call."

Carole wasn't terribly mechanical. She cut Lisa off the first time she tried, and the second time she found herself listening to a recording that told her a phone was off the hook.

"Of course it's off the hook. I'm talking on it," she grumbled back at the recording. But then she wasn't talking on it at all, because she'd been disconnected from both the recording and from Lisa. The third time it worked.

"Hello?" Stevie answered.

"Hi, Stevie, it's Carole."

"And Lisa."

"Hi."

It was very rare for Stevie to have nothing to say but "hi."

"Can you believe that Carole actually figured out how to make a three-way call?" Lisa asked brightly.

"Great," said Stevie.

This was not a good sign. Stevie rarely gave one-word answers to questions. In fact, there were several people who thought she didn't know how to give a one-word answer to anything. She had always been a great talker. Lisa decided to delve further to see what she could find out and what she could do.

"How's Alex doing?" she asked. "At Pine Hollow some of the kids were saying that he's getting better. Is it true?"

"Yes, isn't it wonderful?" Stevie said, now almost breathlessly excited. "He's awake most of the time these days. He doesn't remember anything from the time he was in the coma, but he's feeling better. He's still terribly weak. He can't even sit up in bed. He has lots of tubes still going places—mostly his arms—and they seem to be doing him good. The doctor has the results of all the blood work and the spinal tap. Did I tell you he's had *two* spinal taps? Anyway, all the information the doctor gets says that Alex is responding to the medication they're giving him and he's getting better. Of course, we don't know how *much* better he'll get. The doctor says that a lot of times patients who recover from meningitis don't recover all the way. I mean, they may have some residual problems. That's the way he put it. Alex is going to have bad headaches for a long time. Sometimes they find neurological problems—that means things with the brain. Sometimes deafness, though he seems to be able to hear pretty well, at least when he's awake now."

Stevie went on, and Carole and Lisa were listening. They were glad to have all the information, though it sounded to them almost like a recording. Stevie was reciting facts and figures about Alex and about meningitis at a rate they couldn't possibly absorb. They both felt as though they were getting a lot more answer than their question had warranted. Carole was accustomed to being accused of giving twenty-five-cent answers to nickel questions. Stevie was giving them a full dollar's worth of information!

"Well, I'm awfully glad he's better," Lisa said when

Stevie finally stopped talking. "And you—how are you doing?"

"Fine. I'm fine," said Stevie.

"Really?" Carole asked.

"Of course," Stevie assured her. "Alex is better, so I'm fine. Really."

"Are you coming over to ride soon?" Lisa asked.

"I don't think so," Stevie said. "Not for a while anyway. I want to spend a lot of time with Alex, especially now that he's awake a little. And I've got my homework to do. You know how it is. . . ."

Lisa did know how it was. She often had trouble finding the time to do her homework. It had never been something that concerned Stevie very much, though, so it hadn't occurred to her that Stevie would know how it was. Both she and Carole were surprised by that response.

"Listen, I've got to go now," Stevie said. "Dinner's in a few minutes, and I want to set the table. Then I'm going back over to the hospital."

"Say hi to Alex," Carole said.

"Yes, from me, too," Lisa added.

"I sure will," Stevie promised them. Then she hung up.

There was a silence between Lisa and Carole. There

was so much to say, but neither of them knew what to say about it.

"Who was that we were speaking to?" Lisa asked, putting her finger on it right away.

"Great question," said Carole. "Do you think that maybe the good news is that Alex is getting better, and the bad news is that aliens have come down and occupied Stevie's body? *Want* to set the table? *Find time* for her homework? I mean, those are noble things to do and all that, but hanging up the phone to go set the table isn't exactly like the Stevie we know and love."

"Weird," said Lisa.

"We've got to do something," said Carole.

"Let's talk to Phil," Lisa suggested.

"Hold on," said Carole. Encouraged by her recent success with making a three-way phone call, she did it again. This time she succeeded on the very first try.

"Hi, Phil. This is Carole—"

"And Lisa."

"Oh, I'm so glad you called," he said. "I talked with Stevie last night and I'm worried about her."

"Us, too," said Lisa. "In fact, Carole just suggested that maybe her body's being occupied by aliens!"

Phil didn't laugh at that, and Lisa wondered if he'd had the same thought.

"What can we do for her?" Carole asked.

"Beats me," said Phil. "When I talked to her last night, I told her I'd pick her up for the dance on Saturday, but she said she couldn't go. Alex might come home the next day, and she feels she has to stay home and do things in preparation for his arrival."

"Like what?" Lisa asked. "Make his bed fresh? All night?"

"I couldn't think of what she meant, either," Phil said. "But she seemed determined not to come to the dance—like it's against the law to have fun if your brother's sick."

"She needs our help," said Carole. "But I have no idea what we can do."

"Me neither," agreed Phil. "Based on my conversation with her last night, I'd say that Alex is the only thing on her mind. Our doing something for him might make Stevie feel better."

"Carole? What do you think?" Lisa asked.

Carole found herself having a jumble of emotions. She felt as though she could understand the way Stevie was feeling, because Carole's own mother had been ill for a long time before she'd died. The thing Carole had found the most comforting of all was riding and spending time at the stable. That didn't seem to be what Stevie wanted now, however. All of her attention was focused on Alex. Maybe they could just support that idea.

"I'm not sure," Carole began. "I would have thought horses would help her. They helped *me* when Mom was sick."

"In Stevie's case I would have thought finding ways to get into trouble would be a helpful distraction!" Phil joked. "At the very least a fun dance."

"Maybe the dance is the problem," Lisa suggested. "It seems sort of frivolous to be thinking about a barn dance when Alex is so sick. Maybe we should just cancel it. Max would understand."

"I wouldn't," said Carole. "Life has to go on. It's not fair to Alex or anyone else to use their illness as an excuse to stop living. Canceling the dance isn't the right answer. Not at all."

Lisa was a little surprised at how strongly Carole reacted to her mild suggestion, but she realized that the idea of life continuing was something Carole had learned the hard way and truly believed. It made sense. She could agree with it.

"So, what, then?"

"Maybe we can just focus the dance on Alex a little," suggested Phil.

"You mean like dedicate it to him?"

72

"Sounds kind of corny, but maybe we could have—oh, I don't know—like a dance contest, and whoever wins it could win the right to take some of the decorations from the dance over to Alex when he gets home from the hospital."

There was a moment of quiet. Carole spoke first.

"Phil, you've been spending too much time around Stevie."

"I have?"

"Yes," Lisa agreed. "You're beginning to think like her."

"I am?"

"Yes, and we *love* it," Carole said.

"It's perfect," Lisa agreed. "Now, do you have enough time in the next four days to become an expert dancer so you can win the contest?"

"Me? I don't think so," he said. "Actually, if Stevie's not going, I'm not sure *I* should go."

"Of course you should," said Carole. "Cam will be there, and he'll be very disappointed if you don't show up."

"Alone? It doesn't seem right."

"Not necessarily alone," said Lisa. "I was going to ask Bob Harris, but it turns out his family is going away for the weekend. Why don't we go together? You've helped us with the decorations; you've come up with an ingenious idea to honor Alex. You certainly ought to be there."

"What if I step on your toes?" Phil asked.

"It's a barn dance," Lisa reminded him. "I'm wearing my cowboy boots. I'll just be sure the toes are steel reinforced."

"It's a deal," said Phil. "And thanks for suggesting it. I've missed Stevie this last week or so while she's been so involved with Alex. Talking with you two makes me feel closer to her."

"That's what friends are supposed to do," said Carole.

"And besides, you're in The Saddle Club, and that means we're obligated to help you when you need it."

"Right now I think we all need one another," said Phil.

"If only Stevie could figure that out, too," Carole said.

They chatted a few more minutes, talking about the decorations and the schedule for Saturday night. They agreed to meet at Lisa's house. Carole was staying over there that night anyway, so it made sense to start out together. Finally they hung up the phones, all three of them.

Carole stood up from her father's recliner and

stretched. She hoped that what they were planning for Alex and Stevie would do some good. She didn't like feeling so helpless. It was a familiar and uncomfortable feeling. She was, at least, confident that they weren't doing anything that would hurt. That was a start.

"Hi, Mrs. Reg," said Stevie as she peered into the office at Pine Hollow.

"Stevie, how great to see you! How's Alex doing?"

"He's doing a little better," she said. "The doctor said he could probably come home on Sunday."

"What wonderful news. You must be feeling relieved."

"Yeah, yeah, I am," Stevie told her. "I couldn't go to the hospital this afternoon, so Mom said I should come over here and be with my friends, but I don't see them. Where is everybody?"

"They just left. They talked someone into driving them over to the mall so they could pick up some more red crepe paper, though I doubt there's much left in the world, considering how much they've already used!"

The dance. It was Saturday, two days from now, the day before Alex was to come home. All the time that Alex had been in the hospital, her friends had been working on the decorations and the food for the dance. They'd probably had to work extra hard without her. That was too bad. Stevie was very good at decorations and food. She liked to work on parties, but this was one she was completely missing. She felt a twinge of sadness, but she knew that Alex's health was more important.

"Go see what they've done, dear," said Mrs. Reg. "And it'll be even better by Saturday. You'll love it when you see it then."

"I won't be there," Stevie said. "I have to be with Alex. He's supposed to come home the next day, you know."

"Hmmm," was all Mrs. Reg said.

"I'll go check out the decorations and let you know what I think," said Stevie.

It was just a short walk to the old barn, but it took Stevie quite a while. In the first place, a young-riders class was just letting out, and everybody asked Stevie how Alex was.

By the time she finished explaining it to Jackie and

Amie, May had come along and wanted the same information. Then she saw Max.

"How's Alex?" he asked. She told him.

Two other students in the class asked the same thing. Two other students got the same answer. It was nice that everyone was so concerned, but at the same time Stevie was sick of filling everyone in.

On the way to Topside's stall, Stevie ran into Veronica diAngelo. Much to her own surprise, Stevie was actually relieved to see the snobby girl. Veronica was so self-centered, it wouldn't occur to her to ask about anybody else, especially not the brother of one of the Saddle Club members.

"Stevie!" Veronica said. "How's Alex?"

Stevie sighed with resignation and told her.

Topside seemed glad to see her.

"You're not going to ask me about Alex, are you, boy?" she whispered into his silky ear. He didn't answer, but he didn't ask about Alex, either. She gave him the hug he deserved.

Then she walked over to the old stable where her friends had been working so hard. When she opened the door, she gasped. It was spectacular, and they'd done it completely without her!

They'd stacked all the bales of hay so that they were like a set of bleachers around the dance floor. Then they'd trimmed the bare ends with red and pink crepe paper. From the rafters hung a sparkling mirrored ball as well as dozens of bright red hearts. The dangling hearts and mirrored ball would look wonderful when it was dark outside and the whole place was lit by the spot-lights that had been strategically placed behind the bales of hay.

Stevie felt a pang of sadness and it took her a minute to identify it. All the brightly colored crepe paper and the shiny mirror ball seemed to say that somebody had been having fun—and that somebody was her friends. It should have made her happy to know that her friends were enjoying themselves, but she felt a little cheated. She should have been having fun *with* them. In fact, she was quite certain that if she'd been having the fun with them, they all would have had more fun. That was one of the things Stevie was good at—making something that was fun just be more fun.

Stevie took a deep breath and swallowed. Feeling left out and envious wasn't going to do anybody any good. She reminded herself that right now she had something more important to do than to have fun. She had to take care of Alex. Besides, she reminded herself, one of the nice things about The Saddle Club was that they all helped one another and learned from one another. Obviously her friends had learned a thing or two about festive decorations from her. And it was great that they could do such a fabulous job without her, she decided, walking back toward Mrs. Reg's office.

"How'd you like that?" asked Mrs. Reg.

"It's something," said Stevie. "I used to think I was the best in the world at that sort of thing, but I guess my friends don't need me anymore, don't you think?"

"I doubt that," Mrs. Reg assured her. "So, now, are you looking for a chore to do? There are a few stalls that need mucking out—"

"Actually, I was hoping to ride," said Stevie. "Do you think I could take Topside out? I just took a look at him and he seems a little restless, like a bit of fresh air would do him good."

"You think so?"

"I do," Stevie said.

"Well, I don't know. I don't think Max would want you to ride alone. . . ."

"Not really alone," Stevie said. "After all, Topside will be with me. If anything goes wrong, he can come for help."

"Nice try," said Mrs. Reg. "I'm glad to see you haven't lost your touch." But she smiled at Stevie. "Okay," she relented. "Take Topside out. But the ground's hard, so I don't want you to do any cantering, and watch out when you're trotting. Take all the precautions you're always supposed to take, and then take even more. I'm not convinced this is a good idea for Topside, but I have the feeling you could use some fresh air, so I'm going against my better judgment."

"Thanks, Mrs. Reg. And don't worry. Your judgment's fine," Stevie said. "I'll be super careful."

"You do that. Your mother doesn't want two children in the hospital, now, does she?"

Stevie decided she'd better get Topside tacked up and out of the stable quickly before Mrs. Reg changed her mind. She ducked into the tack room, picked up everything she'd need for a trail ride with Topside, and had him ready in record time. She gave his girth one final tightening tug, mounted up, touched the good-luck horseshoe, and before anyone could think better of letting her take a lone trail ride, she was gone. At a walk.

Stevie pondered Mrs. Reg's admonition about her safety. The words *Your mother doesn't want two children in the hospital now, does she?* kept circling in her mind. She thought about what it would be like if she *were* in the hospital. Alex was getting a lot of attention. Nurses checked him at least once an hour. People stopped by. Friends sent cards and notes. Everyone in their class had made a card for him. His whole karate class had signed a big get-well card. Aunts and uncles seemed to be appearing from out of the woodwork with books, magazines, and bowers of flowers. Three neighbors had brought over covered dishes so nobody in the family would have to cook, and so they could spend more time at the hospital.

All the Lakes were visiting Alex as often as they could, day and night. Stevie and her parents spent the most time there, but Chad and Michael came over every day. They watched Alex when he was sleeping. They asked him what they could do for him when he was awake. They read to him. They changed the television station for him. They fluffed up his pillows.

And he seemed to be loving every minute of it—at least now that he was feeling better. Stevie thought about what it would be like to have people take care of her the way people were taking care of Alex. The other afternoon Alex had said he was hungry for something sweet. Stevie, who happened to have her bike at the hospital, had ridden all the way over to TD's and gotten him hot fudge on chocolate-mint ice cream—his favorite.

If she'd been the one in bed, would he have brought her boysenberry on coffee, with pineapple chunks, M&M's, and walnut sauce? She would have liked that. It certainly would have shown how much he loved her —just as much as she loved him.

Everybody loved Alex. At least everybody asked

about him and really cared about the answers. Today at school she'd been counting. Sixteen people had asked about Alex before lunch. She stopped counting at lunch because a whole bunch of sixth-grade girls asked all at once. Stevie couldn't help but wonder if Alex had started fishing for girlfriends in the classes below them, since he'd been striking out with all the girls in their own class. She'd been a little turned off by the girls' gushy curiosity, and so she'd stopped counting. Still, a lot of people wanted to know how he was doing. Stevie wondered if they'd be asking the same questions if she were the one in the hospital.

"Oh, stop it!" she told herself. "Just because Alex is getting a lot of attention and you're not is no reason to feel sorry for yourself."

She must have unwittingly yanked on the reins in order to underscore her point, because Topside came to a halt.

"Did I do that?" she asked the horse. He didn't answer. "Okay, I'll try not to confuse you again. It's all part of my scheme, you know. I'm working very hard at being a better person. It's all for Alex's sake," she explained to the horse, who listened attentively. "I'm trying to do everything right, but obviously I'm not succeeding totally, since I apparently just made a mistake with you. It wasn't a big mistake, though. It was

just a little mistake. You can forgive me, can't you?"
There was no answer. "Oh, all right. If you can't forgive
me, I'll try to make it up to you by letting you trot.
Want to do that for a little while?"

That was a question Topside could answer. Like most
horses, although he wasn't a very good speaker of English, he'd learned the most important words. "Trot"
was one of them. Without further ado, he picked up the
two-beat gait and Stevie was posting. She knew she'd
made another mistake with Topside, letting him trot
before she'd actually given him the signal with her legs,
feet, seat, and hands. However, he *was* doing what she
wanted, and right now that seemed more important
than correcting a mistake. She let him trot on because
she loved it.

She loved the feel of the powerful, beautiful horse she
was riding. She loved the sense that she was mostly in
charge, even though today he'd trotted before she sig-
naled him. She loved being alone with Topside, able to
talk about whatever she wanted. She loved not having
to pretend anything. And most of all, she loved the fact
that, for a few minutes, she didn't have to worry about
Alex.

Without being particularly aware of it, Stevie found
herself next to the big rock by the creek, where she and

Phil had been sitting when she'd heard the gong from Pine Hollow.

Topside drew to a halt, at Stevie's request. She looked out over the rushing water, the trees bare of their summer leaves, and the pines with their long needles waving softly in the February breeze. The scene was the same as she remembered it, but Stevie felt as if it were the only thing that hadn't changed. Everything else was turning upside down, or going around in circles, or just being different.

Stevie dismounted and secured Topside's reins to a branch. She walked over to the creek and crouched, listening to the rustling water as it followed its path over rocks and around branches—the water ever changing, the path remaining the same. Stevie reached out and let the icy water lap at her fingertips. It was cold, very cold. It numbed her fingers almost immediately, but she left her fingers in the water tingling uncomfortably because that discomfort kept her mind off what was really uncomfortable for Stevie—her confusion. It even kept her mind off the tears that rolled down off her cheeks into the icy water.

9

An hour later Stevie's tears were dried and almost forgotten and she was on her way to the hospital. When she thought about Alex, she felt selfish about her earlier confusion. He was what was important. His health is what mattered and as long as Stevie kept on behaving, he'd be all right. She was sure of that. After all, it was working so far.

Stevie put a smile on her face and walked into the hospital, waving at the receptionist, who, by now, knew her on sight. She felt refreshed and ready to be by her brother's side. She was able to fill her promise to herself and be the kind of person she knew she needed to be in order for Alex to get better. Taking a ride had been a *good* idea, she decided—momentarily forgetting all the anger and resentment that seemed to want to peer out from behind her virtues. It had been especially nice to see her two best friends, if only for a moment.

Stevie took the elevator up to Alex's floor, greeted the nurses, and headed straight for Alex's room. The doctor had said Alex had to remain quarantined until he was ready to go home. That meant they still couldn't be in the room with him. The room had a glass wall so she could look in, and now that Alex was feeling well enough to talk, Stevie could stand at the door and chat with him. She was happy to see him sitting up in bed as she approached. She waved at him. He waved back but he didn't call out, because he was on the phone.

Stevie was struck by the image of him. He sat up in his bed, surrounded by flowers sent by loving, caring friends. Get-well cards covered the walls around his bed, and a bunch of helium-filled balloons dangled their festive ribbons from the ceiling. In the middle of it all Alex looked very small, sitting there with an IV dripping into one arm and the phone cradled against his shoulder. He had to hold the phone that way because he was playing a mini–video game with his hands. The television was showing a *Star Trek* rerun. He had the sound off because he'd seen the show so many times, he didn't even have to listen to it anymore.

"Wait a sec, Josh," he said into the phone. Then he looked up at Stevie. "How ya doin'?" he asked her cheerfully.

"Just fine. Wonderfully, in fact, now that I see how well you're doing."

"I'll be with you in a few minutes. I'm just explaining to Josh what I've learned about this Maxx Racer game. It's awesome."

"No problem. I'll wait," said Stevie. She turned and sat down on the bench. Her routine was so set by now that her mother had come by earlier, bringing her schoolbooks. Her homework was waiting for her while she waited for her brother.

She decided to begin with science. She opened her book to page eighty-seven and found herself staring at a diagram of the human circulatory system with an inset diagram showing how the blood got oxygenated while it zipped through the four chambers of the heart. Her assignment was to make her own diagram of the heart. She took out a pencil and paper and began to draw the outline. Normally, she was pretty good in art and could make a credible diagram of almost anything. Today, however, nothing was working right. Her first attempt came out lopsided. The second try looked too short and squat. She tore up the paper and tried again. This time it was long and seemed more lumpy than anything, but she could probably make a decent diagram out of it. Probably.

She sat up and peered over her shoulder into Alex's room. Maybe he was ready to talk to her by now. He was still on the phone. She turned her attention back to her heart.

"Groan," she said, trying to sort out ventricles.

"What's up?" Beverly asked, sitting down beside Stevie.

"My heart," Stevie began.

"I know," Beverly said. "These are very hard times for you. It must feel as though your heart is breaking. But he *is* getting better, and the tests this afternoon indicate that there will be no residual damage from the disease. The doctor says he's going to make a complete recovery, as long as he takes care of himself now. That should be good news for your heart, right?"

"I suppose," said Stevie. "But that isn't the heart I was talking about. It's this one." She showed Beverly her attempt at drawing a human heart.

"Oh, anatomy was my best subject in nursing school," Beverly said. "Let's see what we can do here. Look, you've got it aimed straight up and down. I think it's easier to draw if you make it a little bit tilted, more like it is in the chest. Here, try this."

Beverly took the pencil and with a few quick strokes

showed Stevie the best way to make her drawing. She'd be able to do it on her own now, but she didn't feel like it. Instead, she drew four concentric Valentine-style hearts.

"That's what we should be working on now, you know," she said to Beverly.

"I think all the patients are getting a few candy hearts on their dinner trays tomorrow," said Beverly. "It's not much, but it does sort of acknowledge a nice holiday."

That sounded nice, but just the thought that the next day was Valentine's Day made her feel that it wasn't enough. "There's a dance Saturday night at the stable where I ride horses," Stevie said.

"I didn't realize you were a rider," said Beverly.

That struck Stevie as very odd. Until Alex had gotten sick, riding was the most important thing in Stevie's life. Since Alex had been admitted to the hospital, she'd literally spent hours talking to Beverly, and she'd never mentioned horses. That didn't seem right at all.

"Yes, and I love it," said Stevie. "I actually was on a trail ride with my boyfriend—he's a rider, too—when I got called to come over here when Alex first got sick."

"Oh, tell me about your boyfriend," said Beverly.

She'd never mentioned Phil, either? And when Stevie thought about it, she realized she'd never mentioned Carole or Lisa. It made her think that the whole wide world had gotten as distorted as her drawing of the heart. Everything that was important had become so unimportant that she hadn't even talked about it.

"So what's his name?"

"Phil," Stevie said. "Phil Marsten. We met at riding camp last summer, and he's so funny and so nice . . ."

She told Beverly all about Phil, and when she was talking about Phil, she also started talking about Lisa and Carole and Pine Hollow and Max and Mrs. Reg. She even told Beverly about Veronica diAngelo. Then she began discussing all the horses at Pine Hollow. It seemed as if she couldn't stop talking. Beverly just listened, very hard.

Stevie paused every few minutes as she talked, glancing into Alex's room to see if he was off the phone yet, but he wasn't. At that moment his life seemed to be his telephone, his television, and his video game. He wouldn't want to hear what Stevie had to say right then, anyway, so Stevie kept on talking to Beverly.

"And what about the dance tomorrow night?" Beverly asked. "What are you going to wear?"

"Oh, it's a barn dance—you know, a square dance," she said. "I've got a real cowboy shirt that I bought when I went out to the dude ranch with Carole and Lisa. I got a hat then, too. It's a little battered, but that's the way they're supposed to be. I mean, if you don't have any dust or dents on your hat, everybody just thinks you're a dude. My hat is battle worn. That proves that I'm a real cowpoke, at least that's what Eli says. He's the wrangler. He even wears a bandanna that he puts over his mouth and nose so he looks like a bank robber, except that it's really just to keep the dust out of his lungs."

"Will you wear one of those, too?" Beverly asked.

"No, of course not," Stevie answered. Then she paused, looking over at her brother, who was still chatting on the phone. "In fact, I won't be wearing any of it, because I'm not going to the dance."

"Why not?"

"Him," Stevie said, pointing at her brother. "A whole bunch of relatives are coming into town for the weekend to see him, and then he's coming home on Sunday, so I have to be home. I can't be thinking of myself all the time, can I?"

It was a pretty good question, and Beverly took a minute to think about it before she answered.

"Not all the time, no," she said, speaking slowly, thoughtfully. "I guess not. But—"

Beverly's answer was interrupted by the beeper that called her to another patient. Stevie knew the answer though.

She couldn't keep on thinking about herself. She had to think about Alex. She had to think about her mother and her father and her other brothers. She shouldn't think about Phil, Carole, Lisa, horses, riding, dances, fun, laughter, enjoyment, tricks, practical jokes, tall tales, or anything else she'd ever liked in her whole life. She had to think about school and homework and Alex. Alex. Alex. The frustrating part was that there he was, not even caring that Stevie was there to see him, that she'd been there to see him for hours every day since he'd first gone into the hospital. She'd sat in that hall and done more boring homework assignments than she ever could have imagined. And he didn't care. All he cared about was a video game and his friend Josh and a stupid old *Star Trek* that he'd already memorized.

Stevie felt totally overwhelmed as she had never felt before. Her world seemed a mass of homework and resentment. Then she felt bad about feeling resentment. Then she felt worse about all the fun she was missing. Then she felt worse still about feeling bad about all the fun she was missing.

She stood up from the bench, grabbed her jacket, and walked, leaving the mess of papers, books, and undone assignments just where they were.

She had to get out of the hospital. Alex didn't need

93

her then. Nobody needed her. She had to leave. She had to go home.

She walked through the hospital door and into the chilly late afternoon before she realized it. She walked all the way home. It was a long walk, more than five miles, but she never noticed any of it. Her parents, Chad, and Michael were all eating dinner when she arrived.

"Stevie, I was going to bring you—" her mother began.

"I don't want any," she said. "I'm not hungry."

"How's Alex?" Chad asked.

"He's gotten to the seventh level of Maxx Racer."

"Stevie, are you—?"

"I'm tired," Stevie said, cutting off her father's question. "I'm going to bed."

"Yo, dork, it's only seven o'clock!" Michael teased her, a little surprised by his sister's behavior. "What are you—some kind of a baby?"

"Then it's almost past your bedtime, *baby* brother," she shot back. It wasn't a very good put-down, but it was the best she could come up with on a second's notice, and it felt good to deliver it to a deserving little brother.

Without further word Stevie ran up to her bedroom and threw herself on her bed. The tears came back then. She was utterly confused by her feelings and even more confused by her confusion. At the time when she should be happy that Alex was getting better, she was getting angry at him for being sick! Or was she angry at him for getting better? Or was she angry at herself? She had no idea. All she knew for sure was that she had spent all her time with her brother, who didn't seem to care, and no time at all with her friends, who seemed to care only about her brother. She wanted everything to be the way it used to be. She wanted to be with Carole and Lisa, and she wanted to be with Phil.

She wanted to go to the dance. She wanted to forget that she'd been sad and worried. She even wanted to forget that she'd done every single assignment from school since Alex had gotten ill!

She reached for her pillow and hugged it tight until the tears slowed down. Then she lay on her bed, exhausted and spent. She looked around her room. Everything there seemed familiar, but not comforting. She'd cried all right, but it hadn't changed anything. She was still unhappy and confused. She looked at her horse posters and the model horses on her bookshelves. She loved them, every one of them. Each was special to her. Then her eyes came to the foil-covered chocolate horse. The repair work she'd done on his leg hadn't held up.

He'd fallen over and gotten even more damaged, smashing his nose when he went.

Stevie stood up from her bed and went to examine him. She'd loved the neat way his ears were so perky and the way his tail fanned out as if brushed by a breeze. A lot of times when people were making horse models of one kind or another, they were sort of phony looking, but not this chocolate horse. He'd been a beauty. Stevie had really loved him. But he didn't look lovable now. He just looked broken down and even a little melted from when Stevie had left him in the window in the sunlight. That part wasn't Alex's fault. She could only blame him for the broken leg. On the other hand, the melted part wouldn't have been so noticeable if it hadn't been for the broken leg. Maybe it *was* Alex's fault. Maybe everything was Alex's fault. Maybe nothing was.

Stevie lay back down on her bed and, finally, fell asleep, exhausted and still confused.

"Wow! We did a wonderful job, didn't we?" Carole asked, walking into the totally transformed feed building. No longer was it a mere shack to hold grains and grass. It was a perfectly decorated old Western dance hall. Everywhere she looked, there were bright red, white, and pink streamers. Red hearts and lanterns hung from the rafters, and the hay bales made perfect benches for kids to sit on when they weren't dancing.

"And look at the food!" Lisa said excitedly. They hadn't been in charge of food. Someone else had done that, and they'd done a wonderful job. Everything was red, white, and pink. There were apples, cherries, fruit punch, cupcakes decorated with pink and red frosting, and even some cookies that had had food dye added to make them pink.

"Not only does it look pretty, it also looks good," Phil said, leading the way to the refreshments.

"Except for the pink cookies," said Cam. "I just can't get too excited about pink chocolate-chip cookies."

"Until you have a taste," Carole said, nibbling cautiously at one. "They taste just like the real thing."

Cam tried one and relented, agreeing that they did, at least, *taste* good.

"Wait until our St. Patrick's Day dance and they all turn green," said Lisa. "Those take a lot more courage to taste."

"I'll pass," Cam said.

"All the more for the rest of us," Phil said brightly.

That remark made Lisa smile. It was exactly the kind of thing Stevie would have said. She missed Stevie. She and Carole had missed Stevie a lot over the last ten days. Lisa loved being with Carole, and Carole loved being with Lisa, but each knew that when Stevie was with them, they had more fun. They also suspected that Stevie had more fun when she was with both of them. Carole and Lisa had talked about it as they were getting ready for the dance that afternoon, and they'd agreed together that, when it came to The Saddle Club, the three of them together were better than each of them apart. Or, as Lisa had put it, the sum was greater than the parts.

Carole had liked that idea. It was a way of saying how important The Saddle Club was to each of them. Being together had a way of bringing out the best in each of them. Now, however, they weren't together. They were still apart, and Lisa and Carole both missed Stevie and wished they'd succeeded in talking her into coming to the dance. So did Phil, but there didn't seem to be any point in dwelling on it.

"Come on, now," Phil said, as if he'd been reading their minds. "Let's focus on having fun tonight. And unless my ears deceive me, I do believe I hear a fiddle warming up. I think it's about time for the first dance to begin."

Phil was right. They finished their cups of fruit punch and headed for the center of the dance floor, where a lot of kids were getting ready for the dance to begin. The four of them found two other couples and made a square with them.

The caller demonstrated all the moves he'd be calling by, temporarily partnering up with Lisa. It didn't look terribly complicated until he added: "Of course, you all will be doing this at about six times the speed we've just done it."

In a matter of seconds the dancers started whirling

around the floor, shaking hands, going in opposite circles, swinging around, first one way, then another, ducking under joined hands and skipping every which way. When the music finally stopped, Carole was breathless.

"It seemed like it was going to be impossible," Carole said. "But it didn't turn out to be so hard."

"Except for the part where you were going the wrong way, you mean," Phil teased.

"Lisa did it first!"

"Yeah, I did," Lisa confessed. "But I was just testing."

She had another chance to "test" a few minutes later when they did another dance, this time more complicated, and more fun. It seemed to Lisa that the whole room whirled with the excitement of the dance and the confusion of attempts to follow the caller's instructions. She loved every minute of it and had to agree with an earlier observation from Stevie that Phil was a marvelous dancer.

Then the four of them sat down on the bales of hay for a few minutes to catch their breath.

"Everybody looks so wonderful," Cam observed. "And so different."

It was true. At Pine Hollow almost all the riding that was done was English riding. English riders sometimes had a bad habit of thinking that their way of riding was "better" than Western riding. The Saddle Club had learned that one way wasn't at all better than the other. They were really just different. And when it came right down to it, they weren't even all that different, because they had a lot more in common than not. Looking at the crowd at Pine Hollow that night, Carole and Lisa realized that there was a little more respect for Western styles and ideas than they had thought. It seemed that everybody had jeans, cowboy boots, and a Western shirt on. The girls who weren't wearing jeans were wearing big circular skirts with puffy crinolines underneath. One of the girls wore a girl's riding skirt. It had a wide split skirt and was edged with a buckskin fringe.

"I don't think I've ever seen so many string ties in one room before," Cam remarked, tugging idly with the strings on his tie as he spoke.

"I'm sorry Stevie isn't here to see this," said Carole. "She's always been a big one for costume parties, and this definitely qualifies as that."

Lisa was going to agree, but she got interrupted when the caller announced the start of a Virginia reel.

For that dance the caller decided to pair everybody up differently. He had the boys make a small circle, and the girls a larger circle outside the smaller circle. They danced in opposite directions until the music stopped and then they were each facing their new partners. Lisa thought of it as a sort of "Musical Partners." She'd been having fun dancing with Phil, but she was very aware of the fact that he was Stevie's boyfriend, and if she danced with him exclusively all night, some people might get the wrong idea. She found herself dancing with Adam Levine for the Virginia reel and then with Joe Novick for the square dance that followed. It wasn't until almost halfway through the evening that Phil found her and brought her over to the bale of hay that they'd staked out for themselves earlier.

"It's almost time for the contest dance," Phil said. "I think we should be partners for that."

"And I think we should win," Lisa agreed. "After all, who better to take flowers, balloons, and hearts over to the Lakes' house than you and me?"

"Not so fast there," said Carole. "There's no guarantee at all that you're going to win. Cam and I have been doing a pretty darn good job on the dance floor. I think you'll find some stiff competition from us."

"Not if it's another reel dance," Lisa said. "I was absolutely wonderful doing it."

"You were? I didn't see you at all," Carole said.

"That's what I mean," Lisa teased. "I was going so fast, you couldn't even see me."

Both Carole and Lisa knew the joking was all in fun.

If either of them won the dance contest, *both* of them would take the balloons to Alex. They knew that.

The caller picked up his microphone and tapped into it. "May I have your attention, please," he began. That meant this definitely was the contest dance. He explained about Alex, although everybody there already knew, but not everybody knew he was coming home from the hospital the next day. There was a joyful cheer when the man gave the dancers that news. Then he explained about the dance contest.

"So, now, everybody get your best partner and let's begin. However, I must tell you my throat is a little tired, so I'm going to sit this one out. The dance contest is going to be a twist!"

Carole's face lit up. Carole's father was a nostalgia buff, and his favorite nostalgic time was the fifties and sixties. His favorite nostalgic dance was the twist. He'd taught Carole how to do it almost before she could walk. Nobody, but nobody, was better at it than she was.

"Did you plan this?" Lisa asked suspiciously.

"*Moi?*" Carole asked, mustering her most innocent look. It made Lisa laugh. She knew Carole hadn't had anything to do with the dance selection. It was just really good luck.

The band got into it, and the caller, in spite of his

protestations of a sore throat, began singing "The Twist."

Carole was in her element—almost as comfortable dancing this dance as she was on horseback. She began at once and didn't miss a beat. Cam did everything to keep up with her, and at the very least did his best to stay out of her way. She pivoted on her toes, first rising, then lowering herself as if she were crouching except that she kept her back straight, then she rose again and began circling Cam, still twisting to the very familiar music.

It really wasn't a contest. By the second verse of the song everybody on the floor had relented and given the floor over to Carole and Cam, allowing Carole a lot more dancing space to strut her stuff, and she did just that.

Lisa was the one who started clapping to the music. Soon all the other onlookers had joined in. It seemed to inspire Carole all the more. As the band neared the end of "The Twist," they couldn't bear to stop watching the floor show Carole was putting on, and they slipped right into "Let's Twist Again," Chubby Checker's follow-up hit to the original twist. Like the band, Carole just kept right on going. And then, when the final note was sounded, she grabbed Cam's hand, looked up at the crowd around her, and asked, "Is it over already?"

She got the round of applause she deserved. Lisa ran out onto the floor and gave her a great big hug.

"I'm coming with you tomorrow morning," she said, as if Carole hadn't already known that.

"But first we'd better call Stevie and let her hear the good news," Phil suggested.

Carole just nodded. Although she hated to admit it, she was totally out of breath. She and Cam shook hands with the caller who told her he'd never seen anyone dance the twist that well. Carole told him that meant he hadn't ever met her father!

"Well, he should be proud of you. You were great out there!"

"I had good reason to be," Carole explained. "See, Alex's sister, Stevie, is my best friend. I was doing it for her."

"Then she should be proud of you, too," he said.

Carole thought Stevie probably would be, and now she couldn't wait to talk to her.

Phil provided the change and placed the call. It took a few minutes to get Stevie on the phone. It seemed that there were a lot of relatives visiting at the Lakes, and the one who answered the phone didn't know exactly where Stevie was. It took four cousins to find someone who knew exactly where she was, and then it took a while for her to find exactly where the phone was, since one of her cousins had moved the phone from her bedside table to the closet so he could make a private phone call. Stevie was pretty steamed by the time she picked up the phone.

"Hi, Stevie, it's Phil," he said, glad to hear her voice after all.

"Hi," she said.

The change in Phil's face when he heard Stevie's voice told Lisa and Carole that something was wrong.

"Is Alex okay?" Phil asked.

"Of course Alex is okay," Stevie said. "Is that why you called? Alex is coming home tomorrow. He'll have to spend another two to three weeks at home in bed, being waited on hand and foot because he can't get overtired or he could get sick all over again. But as long as we take good care of him—*really* good care of him— he's going to be good as new. That's how Alex is."

"Um, we're calling you from the dance," Phil said. "Lisa and Carole are here. We wanted to talk to you, and we've got some news for you, too. At least Lisa and Carole were here a second ago. Let me get them. I know they want to talk to you."

Since both Lisa and Carole were standing right next to him, that was a very odd statement for him to make to Stevie. Obviously, he needed to talk to them before they talked to Stevie.

He covered the phone with his hand. "She's down in the dumps," he said. "Really upset."

"Alex?" Carole whispered the question.

"He's fine. It's Stevie who isn't. Good luck." He handed the phone to Carole. She and Lisa did the best they could to share it.

"Hi, Stevie, we miss you," Lisa said.

"I bet you're having a good time."

"Not as good a time as we'd be having if you were here," Carole assured her.

"Oh, I don't know about that," said Stevie glumly. "I'm really not much fun these days."

"Stevie!" Lisa said, almost shocked by Stevie's statement. If there was one thing that could *always* be counted on it was that Stevie was fun.

"It's just that there's so much—you know—" Stevie said.

Her friends weren't at all sure they *did* know, but they also knew that there were times when it was pointless to argue with Stevie, and this appeared to be one of them.

"So much Alex," Stevie said, completing her sentence after a pause.

"Yeah," said Carole softly.

"Carole just won a twist contest," Lisa began, about to tell Stevie that they'd bring the balloons over tomorrow. But Carole shook her head warningly, and Lisa immediately caught on. Maybe this wasn't the best time to be talking about Alex.

"I wish I could have seen the contest," said Stevie wistfully.

Lisa didn't know what to say back. Obviously there was just about nothing she and Carole could say that would cheer their friend up.

"Here's Phil again," Carole said. She handed the phone to Phil, who said just a few more things to Stevie before hanging up.

The three of them and Cam stood looking at one another.

"She's in trouble," said Carole.

"Big time," Phil agreed.

"Major league."

"We've got to do something for her," Lisa said.

"Definitely," said Carole. "In fact, I'm beginning to get the feeling that this is a Saddle Club project."

Lisa nodded. It had all the earmarks of one. Since the second requirement for membership was helping out other members—even when they didn't know they needed help—it was time for them to join together and help Stevie. She definitely needed it, so badly that she didn't even know.

"Time for a Saddle Club meeting," Lisa declared. Carole agreed totally.

11

"ISN'T THIS CALLED breaking and entering?" Lisa whispered to Carole.

"Not when it's your best friend's house and you're coming over here to bring her something, not steal something," Carole answered her, using Stevian logic. "And besides, the back door was open."

The two of them slipped in through the kitchen door —the one they knew was always left open after six-thirty in the morning when Mr. Lake went for his morning run.

They had to be very quiet because they didn't want to wake anybody up, and it wasn't easy being quiet when they were carrying so much stuff.

First of all, there were the balloons and the hearts from the dance for Alex. Carole tiptoed upstairs to Alex's room, now empty and clean, waiting for his return from the hospital later in the morning. This was the last time she was going to think about Alex while they were there. She and Lisa had made an agreement that this morning's surprise was totally about *Stevie*. They'd promised one another they wouldn't even mention Alex's name while they were with Stevie.

Carole deposited the balloons and hearts in Alex's room, then crept back downstairs to help Lisa assemble their surprise for Stevie.

"I wish Phil could be here with us," Lisa said.

"Me too," Carole agreed. "But there was no way he was going to convince either of his parents to drive him over here at this hour to have breakfast with his girl-friend."

"It does sound kind of funny, I guess," Lisa said. "Still, he really belongs here. This is a Saddle Club project, and he is part of The Saddle Club."

"Well, there's no point in worrying about that now. We've got a job to do even without Phil's help."

They got to work.

The girls had spent enough time at the Lakes' to know where the plates, bowls, and glasses were. It took them only a few minutes to set up a tray. It took a little longer to put all the food on it.

First of all, there were the beverages. The girls weren't sure whether Stevie would prefer milk or orange juice for her breakfast in bed, so they'd brought both. Then they'd agreed right away that cold cereal was just too boring, so they'd made some pancakes. Now they warmed them up in the Lakes' microwave. They looked a little limp, but they were sure they would taste good. Lisa applied butter. Carole poured on the syrup. There were two slices of bacon and half a grapefruit. Lisa had wanted half a maraschino cherry to put over the center of the grapefruit because that always looked so pretty, but there wasn't a maraschino cherry to be had anywhere in the Atwood kitchen. Carole had located a red pepper and sliced off a circular chunk. It wouldn't taste like a maraschino cherry, but, the girls agreed, it *looked* just as pretty. They'd brought a knife, fork, and spoon from Lisa's house. They took a napkin from the Lakes' napkin rack. All of this was put on a tray.

Then came their favorite part. While Stevie had been so busy taking care of and worrying about Alex, her friends had missed her terribly all the time, but most especially when they'd gone to TD's for ice cream. They were pretty sure she'd missed them, too, and they were absolutely certain she'd missed having one of her fa-

112

mous TD's ice-cream sundaes. They hadn't been able to get to TD's, but they were confident they'd come close to imitating the kind of thing Stevie usually ate while she was there. They were both glad that Mrs. Atwood seemed to have a passion for fruit preserves. It was just what they needed.

They'd begun with vanilla frozen yogurt. That was a lot more normal than what Stevie usually chose, but it was the only thing that approached ice cream in the Atwood freezer—except for a little glob of pistachio ice cream that Lisa swore had been there since before she'd been born. They'd resisted the temptation to add that. Then came the chocolate sauce. Next, a dash of orange marmalade followed by red raspberry sauce. They couldn't find any pineapple sauce, but they found some pineapple chunks. They added those. Then they located some peanuts and chopped walnuts. There wasn't any whipped cream, but there was a container of nondairy dessert topping. To that they'd added a few sugar fancies, some cinnamon hearts, and to top it all off, a small chunk of sweet red pepper. Carole had reminded Lisa that Stevie *always* asked for a maraschino cherry on top of her sundaes, and since they'd used the pepper on the grapefruit in place of a cherry, it would be nicely consistent to put one on the sundae.

Now Lisa placed the sundae on the tray and the girls

stood back and looked at the concoction. It looked absolutely and totally revolting. They were sure Stevie would love it.

"I'll carry the tray; you lead the way," Carole said.

Lisa looked to be sure the kitchen was as tidy as they'd found it, and together the girls tiptoed to the staircase.

They were good at tiptoeing around the Lakes' house. They'd both slept over there often, and staying at Stevie's house usually involved tiptoeing someplace they weren't supposed to be. The girls knew the creaky spots on the staircase almost as well as Stevie did.

In a matter of seconds they were up the stairs and outside Stevie's room.

Lisa turned the knob and went in. Carole followed. Lisa flipped on the wall switch.

Stevie's eyes popped open. "What the—?"

"Surprise!" Carole and Lisa said in a single voice.

"Huh?"

"We brought you breakfast in bed," said Lisa.

"Whuh?"

"We decided that you needed to be treated just a little bit like the wonderful person you are for at least a morning, so we made you a royal treat."

"Wha?"

Stevie was slow to wake up. She always was that way,

and her friends always knew it. They were patient, though, and they didn't mind explaining again once Carole had put the heavy tray down on Stevie's bureau.

"We haven't seen you," Carole said. "We just needed to spend some time with you, so we decided to kill two birds with one stone."

"What Carole means," Lisa jumped in, "is that we wanted to do something nice for you *and* do something nice for us. For you we made breakfast. For us we planned a visit with you. So, surprise!"

Slowly but surely, it began sinking in through the cobwebs that seemed to be covering Stevie's brain.

"How'd you . . . What'd you?"

Carole knew how to answer those questions. "We came in through the back door after your father went for his morning run. We brought breakfast over from Lisa's house, where I spent the night last night after the dance."

"Oh, right, the dance," Stevie said, looking sad.

"So are you ready for breakfast?" Lisa chimed in cheerfully.

Stevie sat up in bed, adjusted the covers, and allowed her friends to bring the tray.

"Oh, goody, just what I was hungry for," Stevie said, long before she actually focused on anything on the tray. "You've made me some—*what?*"

"Breakfast," Lisa said as if that could explain what Stevie was looking at.

Then as the whole meal came into focus, Stevie began giggling. "The pancakes and bacon look delicious," she said, taking a little taste. "Taste delicious, too. And as you know, I do love grapefruit. But what's this other stuff?"

"Dessert," Carole explained. But she really didn't have to explain it. Stevie knew exactly what it was. She recognized one of her TD's concoctions, even with a chunk of red pepper where a maraschino cherry ought to be.

Stevie's giggles continued. As far as Lisa and Carole were concerned, that was the nicest sound they'd heard for almost two weeks, and they hadn't even known how much they'd missed it.

"Oh, Stevie!" Lisa began.

"We've missed you so much!" Carole added.

"And I—I—" Stevie couldn't talk. She also couldn't believe what a nice, thoughtful, kind, loving thing her friends had done for her just because they missed her. She'd been so busy worrying about Alex and being a perfect person that she'd almost forgotten how much fun it was to be with them. But right now she was overwhelmed by her happiness at seeing her friends, even at this ridiculous hour of the day and accompanied by the revolting sundae. "I . . . I," she began again. Then she finished with, "I don't think I can eat this sundae right now."

That made Lisa and Carole laugh, and their laughter made Stevie all the happier to see them.

"No problem. I'll just stick this into the freezer, and you can have it whenever you want it. It will be waiting for you," Lisa said brightly, whisking it away before it began to melt onto something important, like the grapefruit.

"Thanks," said Stevie, settling into the pancakes, which did taste good even if they were a little limp.

"So, tell me *everything*," Stevie said when Lisa returned from the freezer.

The girls began. First, they knew Stevie would want to know about the dance, but they were also sensitive to the fact that if it sounded *too* wonderful, she might feel all the more miserable about missing it.

"The band was pretty good, and it was fun to do square dances," Lisa began.

"Except that they make you very tired and you run out of breath," Carole added.

"How was Phil?"

They knew they could be as enthusiastic as they wanted about Phil. "You're so lucky, Stevie," said Lisa.

"He was great. He's lots of fun to be with, and he's a wonderful dancer."

"But he never stopped talking about you," Carole said.

"Right. It was his idea to call you last night. He paid for it, too."

"I'm glad you guys called, though I don't think I was in a very good mood. I wasn't much fun to talk to."

"You haven't been having much fun," Carole said. "No wonder you're not feeling very fun."

"But we're having fun now, aren't we?" Lisa asked. "And you would have had fun last night if you'd been there to see Carole and Cam dance together in the contest, not that Cam danced much. Carole did it all by herself."

"I wish I'd been there," Stevie said. "Your dad taught me how to do that dance, too. I would have given you a run for your money."

"And I would have liked that. Now, if only *Dad* could have been there."

"What was the contest anyway?" Stevie asked.

Lisa answered immediately. "Just a contest," she said. "Carole got some of the decorations from the dance. Balloons and stuff, you know."

"Oh," Stevie said. "I was hoping it would be a trip for three to someplace exotic."

"Right," said Carole.

"No, that's the way it should be. Like, if you win a waltz contest, you should get a trip to Vienna; a cha-cha gets you to Havana; the mambo to—I don't know, where was that invented?"

"And a twist contest gets you a trip in a time machine back to the sixties?"

"Perfect!" said Stevie.

It made Lisa and Carole happy to hear Stevie chattering like that. That was *Stevie*. She was reverting to her lovable old self again. The breakfast in bed was working.

Before long they were all talking completely normally. Carole and Lisa didn't have to remind themselves not to talk about Alex, because normally they didn't talk about Alex. They talked about horses and Pine Hollow.

They brought Stevie up-to-date on all the horses and people at the stable. One of the ponies had a slightly sore leg, and the Pony Club Horse Wise was using that as a model to practice bandaging legs.

"Poor old Nickel has that leg rebandaged five or eight times a day."

"It's a good thing it's not very sore," said Carole. "Otherwise it wouldn't be good for him to remove the bandage all the time."

"Right. Judy said it didn't even really need a bandage. Max is just using it as an excuse for the little kids to study bandaging techniques," Lisa explained.

"But you should have been there when he asked Veronica to bandage the leg," said Carole.

"Oh, let me guess! She didn't want to do it because Nickel isn't a Thoroughbred!" Stevie said.

"How'd you figure that out?" Lisa asked, genuinely impressed that Stevie had gotten it right. "In fact, she asked Max to check with Judy to find out if the pony's leg was the same as that of the purebreds she was accustomed to riding and caring for."

"I bet Max was furious!" Stevie said, her eyes brightening with glee at the image.

"His face turned bright red," said Lisa.

"We didn't know whether he was angrier that Veronica would have such a stupid snobby attitude toward horses—"

"Or because Veronica had suggested that *he* wouldn't know the answer to the question!" Lisa finished.

"Oh, I wish I could have been there!"

"Us, too," Carole said. "We've missed you. Really."

"A lot," said Lisa.

"I know. I've missed you, too. But I'm not sure I knew how much I missed you until right now." Stevie was on the verge of getting sentimental again, and she knew it.

She reached for her grapefruit and ate a couple of the sections. Then she slid her spoon under what she presumed was a cherry in the middle of it and put it in her mouth.

Lisa and Carole waited, wondering.

She spat it out. "That's not a cherry."

"Red pepper," Carole told her. "We didn't have a cherry. We did the best we could."

"On the sundae, too?" Stevie asked.

"Yup," Lisa told her.

Stevie's eyes narrowed. "You guys haven't missed me at all," she said. "You've done exactly all the things *I* would have done, and I'm proud of you because it means I've taught you well."

Carole and Lisa couldn't help themselves then. They each gave Stevie a big hug, and she hugged them back. It was a way to keep from saying what was on all of their minds, and that was all right, because none of that needed to be said anyway.

In a minute they were back to talking about horses and were deeply involved in a discussion of techniques to control a stubborn horse. Stevie thought it was most important to get him calmed down before giving him any instructions. Carole suggested that it might make more sense to give him lots of instructions—so many that it would keep his mind off what it was he'd wanted to do in the first place. Lisa thought both techniques were worth trying.

There was a knock at Stevie's door. It was Stevie's mother, and she was more than a little surprised to see Lisa and Carole sitting on Stevie's bed and a tray across Stevie's lap.

"We brought her breakfast in bed," Carole explained. She felt a little bad about having sneaked into the house and was going to apologize for it, but the smile on Mrs. Lake's face told her no apology was necessary.

"Good," she said. "If I'd thought of it, I would have done the same thing. She deserves it. However, I suspect that whatever you made for her tasted better than anything I might have thought of."

"We hope you don't mind," Lisa said.

"Not at all," Stevie's mother said. Then she turned to Stevie. "We'll be leaving in about an hour to bring Alex home. Will you be ready by then?"

Stevie found herself almost a little surprised. Of course, she knew Alex was coming home today, but she'd forgotten about it temporarily. She'd been having such a nice time with Lisa and Carole that all her sadness and confusion had been swept under the table. But here it was again. Alex. Alex was coming home.

"I don't think so, Mom," she said. "I think I'll just wait here. Do you mind?"

"Uh, no," said Mrs. Lake, clearly more surprised than upset. "I just thought, well, there's going to be a lot to carry, flowers and everything, you know."

"Chad and Michael can help, and don't we have fourteen zillion cousins here now?"

"Three today," said Mrs. Lake. "Just three."

"I'd rather wait here," Stevie said.

"Okay, sure," said her mother. "I understand. You have something special planned for him, don't you?"

"I'll be here," Stevie said again, avoiding her mother's question.

The door closed, and the three friends were alone again. Stevie spoke first.

"You know, Carole, I think you're right. The last time Topside was being fussy, I actually started giving him orders, and he followed them until I figured he'd forgotten what it was he was being fussy about. I guess I'll stick with that technique."

They were back to their favorite subject: horses.

CAROLE AND LISA stayed for another hour, and then they had to return to Lisa's house because they needed to change into their riding clothes. They were going to do some chores at Pine Hollow because Max had said if they got enough done, they could go for a trail ride later. They asked Stevie if she'd like to come along, but she said she thought she probably shouldn't. They understood. Stevie told them to have fun and thanked them again for her wonderful surprise breakfast.

Then everything was quiet in her room and in her house. Everybody else had gone to the hospital to get Alex. He'd be back here in a little while, and Stevie found that unsettling. She'd almost gotten used to her routine of going straight to the hospital after school, finishing her homework, and then coming home. That's what seemed like normal now. Did that mean she'd have to get used to a new normal?

She decided to worry about that later and found that decision comforting in itself. It was very much like Stevie—the real Stevie—to put off a decision.

In the quiet of the house, Stevie's mind wandered back over the events since Alex had gotten sick. She recalled her trip to the hospital with Mrs. Reg and the rambling tale Mrs. Reg had told about the two horses who'd been separated. The trick to Mrs. Reg's stories was to figure out what they were really about. In this case Stevie thought she knew. Mrs. Reg was telling her that it was important for her to be with Alex—that she was a better person when she was with Alex. At least, that's what she *thought* Mrs. Reg's story was about. Sometimes, of course, they weren't about anything. They were just stories.

A car pulled up in front of the garage, then another one. Car doors started opening and slamming shut. Alex was home. So were the rest of the Lakes and the visiting cousins. Quiet time was over.

A part of Stevie thought she ought to be running down to greet her brother, to carry his suitcase, his flowers, his get-well cards. She should turn down his bed, bring him a pitcher of water, put his favorite comic books by his bed.

She stayed in her room, sitting on her own bed, thinking. She heard voices, cheerful, relieved, welcoming, just the way they ought to sound. She even heard Alex's voice, saying how glad he was to be home.

"Where's Stevie?" he asked.

"Somewhere," Chad answered.

"I think she has something special planned for you," Mrs. Lake said. "She'll show up soon, I know. Now, it's time for you to get into bed and to rest. We'll make some lunch and bring it up in a little while, okay?"

"Okay."

There were more fussing sounds, and then Alex's door was opened and closed and feet shuffled along the hallway and down the stairs. Then there was quiet.

Stevie didn't move.

She could hear cheerful family sounds downstairs, sounds of her mother making soup and sandwiches while the cousins opened and closed cabinet doors in the kitchen, looking first for the soup bowls, then for the proper silverware. Upstairs, nobody spoke.

Stevie found herself thinking about Alex's illness and her reaction. She thought about all the assignments she'd done, all the good, virtuous acts she'd committed, all the silly things she'd resisted doing, all the fun she'd missed. Now that Alex was definitely better and was soon going to be completely better, her vow of perfection seemed a little silly—almost as silly as the eruption of anger and resentment that had come over her so recently.

Stevie shook her head in annoyance at herself. She wasn't a perfect person. She wasn't an evil, angry person, either. She was Stevie, and although that fact often seemed to get her into trouble, on the whole she rather liked herself. Her friends did, too. There had to be a happy medium somewhere. She just wasn't sure exactly where that somewhere was.

There was a knock at her door.

"Come in," she said, expecting to see her mother. Instead, it was Alex.

"You okay?" he asked.

"Me? Of course. You're the one who's been sick. You should be in bed, resting."

"I'm tired of resting," he said. "I feel pretty good. I think I can be up for a little while anyway."

"I think Mom'll kill you if she finds you're out of bed, so why don't you come sit on mine? That's almost as good, isn't it?"

"Sure," he said, and he sat down next to her, accepting her offering of pillows. "So what's been going on at school?" he asked.

"Mostly it's been people asking about you. If you ever get the idea that no one cares about you, just ask me. I've been telling a zillion people about you every single day. Everybody asks—I mean *everybody*. I actually have had eight conversations with Miss Fenton that didn't have to begin 'Let me explain my side . . .' "

Alex laughed. Stevie was famous for explaining things so people would see them her way. It was her favorite technique for getting out of hot water.

"At least my getting sick has had one advantage for you," Alex teased. "But how are you doing? I've been worried about you."

"You, worried about me?" Stevie asked.

"Yeah, sure," he said. "Beverly, the nurse, told me you were there at the hospital every afternoon, working on your homework. Naturally, I thought she was joking. I told her that maybe you'd been drawing pictures of horses or rereading *Misty of Chincoteague* or something, but not homework. Then Friday, when you left your book bag, Beverly brought it into my room. I took a look because I thought it would be a good idea to see what I've been missing. And what do I see?"

"What?" Stevie asked.

"No horse pictures, no *Misty*. All I see is homework papers without 'Late' written up at the top. They all have really good grades, too. And they're in your handwriting. And so I ask myself, 'Has Stevie had a personality transplant? And if so, how am I going to learn to live with it, and who's going to tell me how to get out of trouble when *I* get into hot water?' "

Stevie didn't have to answer the question; he didn't really expect an answer anyway. It was just nice to have him home and well, and she was surprised to find that all her concern about her own confusing behavior didn't need an explanation—at least not to her twin brother.

They began chatting. Stevie told him more about things that were going on at school, some things that they'd been learning and that she'd help him catch up on. She also told him about the dance at Pine Hollow the night before.

"Oh, that explains the balloons and hearts in my room," Alex said. "There was a note on them from Carole. That was very nice of her."

"Yes, it was," Stevie said, though she was surprised. Carole and Lisa hadn't said anything about bringing balloons and hearts for Alex. She smiled to herself, though, understanding that her friends had worked very hard to make this morning's treat be for and about *her*. They were very good friends, indeed.

"Well, then this morning when they brought the balloons for you, they brought *me* breakfast in bed."

"Really?"

"And you won't believe what they brought me, either." She tried to describe the sundae, and just talking about it made her mouth water.

"Sounds wonderful," said Alex. It seemed that being twins gave them a few things in common that nobody could have anticipated.

"Yeah, I wish I had it right now," Stevie said.

"Me, too. I'm hungry."

"Mom's making lunch," Stevie reminded him.

"No, I mean I'm hungry for real food—like a good sundae, you know, something sweet."

Stevie shook her head. "No way. Mom would freak out if I brought you that before you had lunch."

She looked around her room to see what she might have that was edible and sweet. "The horse," she said. "The chocolate horse." It was there, still on her windowsill and looking very unhealthy. All the leg wraps Horse Wise could devise wouldn't cure what ailed him. Stevie stood up and went to get the poor old horse.

"No," Alex said. "I couldn't. You shouldn't, either. You don't have to, I mean. I never should have tried to eat it. Put it back, Stevie."

But there was no stopping Stevie. She was hungry,

Alex was hungry, and the horse was there, useless as a decoration, ready to be eaten. Somehow it seemed like the most right thing in the world to share the melted chocolate horse with her brother, right then, right there.

"We shall dine," she said, unwrapping the twisted foil.

"I ruined it," said Alex.

"I don't think so," Stevie told him. "I think he got ruined because I left him by the window in the sun. You probably didn't help him, but it was my mistake in the first place."

"We shouldn't eat it. He's special to you."

"He isn't special. He isn't even a 'he.' It's an 'it,' and it's candy, and it's time for a treat—if only I hadn't put it *back* in the sunlight, because it's pretty gooey."

"Just the way I like it," Alex said, relenting. "Here, I think there's an end of the foil here, and if we tug at it just the right way—"

It worked. In a matter of seconds the foil was completely off, and the twins had found a way to share the candy relatively equally. It was very good milk chocolate—just the very thing that Stevie and Alex were both hungry for.

When the last bit of chocolate was gone and the last

finger licked clean, Stevie said, "I think it's time for you to get back into bed and get some rest."

"I think you're right," he said. "And I think it's time for you to return to normal and stop trying to be perfect."

"I think you're right," she said.

13

"Do my eyes deceive me, or is that Stevie Lake climbing out of a car?" Carole asked Lisa, peering through the dusty window of a freshly mucked-out stall.

"Wearing riding clothes!" Lisa added excitedly. "She's going to come with us on our trail ride!"

"And she's absolutely back to normal because she's arrived here at the exact second when we've finished doing all the work!" Carole said.

Lisa knew she was just joking. Stevie had a million ways to wriggle out of doing work, but not when the work came to horses. She was always willing to do something at the stable.

"Is it too late, or can I come along?" Stevie asked, when her friends greeted her at the door with big hugs.

"Of course it's not too late, and of course you can come along," Carole assured her. "We just have to do a little more work taking down decorations from the dance. Come help, will you?"

"Definitely," Stevie said.

The three of them went over to the scene of the Valentine's dance, where most of the decorations were still in evidence.

"You lied to me," Stevie accused them. "I can just tell looking at this stuff that you guys really had a wonderful time. Didn't you?"

"Yeah, we did," Lisa confessed. "The dance was totally great. The part we didn't lie about, though, was that it would have been more fun if you'd been here."

"We just didn't want you to feel sad and sorry for yourself," said Carole.

"That's what friends are for," Stevie confirmed. "I'd do the same for you, too. But don't worry about me. I called Phil after lunch and already told him that I'll be here next Valentine's Day and it'll be even more fun. Now we have the fun of ripping all this stuff down. I got dibs first on the ladder!"

In contrast to the days and hours it had taken to put all the decorations up, it took only a very few minutes to take them down, and just a few minutes after that for the girls to tack up their horses, touch the good-luck horseshoe, and aim themselves for the trail.

Stevie didn't think that anything had ever felt so good as being on horseback riding with her friends, and she started to tell them so but decided against it, thinking they probably already knew that, anyway.

The horses seemed as glad to be out of the stable and on the trail as the girls were. It was a very warm day for February, suggesting an early spring. That was something else to look forward to as far as the riders were concerned.

Before too long the girls were at the edge of Willow Creek. They secured their horses and climbed up onto their favorite rock. Stevie couldn't resist. She took off her boots and her socks and dangled her toes in the water.

"Stevie!" Lisa said. "That stuff's cold."

"Feels great," Stevie insisted, though she did take her feet out rather quickly. It didn't make Carole and Lisa want to put theirs in. It did, however, remind them how glad they were that they had a friend who could do silly things—and then deny that they were silly.

"Did you eat the sundae?" Lisa asked.

"Every bite," Stevie said. "Except that I shared it with Alex. He loved it, too."

"You mean weird taste buds are genetic?" Carole asked.

"Maybe, but Chad and Michael didn't want any. Actually, that's not true. Michael begged me for the cherry. I told him he couldn't have it, and then I turned away for a minute, and guess what, he took it. I knew he would. And, of course, it tasted weird, but he couldn't admit he'd stolen it, so he couldn't admit it tasted weird. It was a fine sibling moment! Thank you guys for making it possible."

"Oh, you're more than welcome," Carole said. "But I don't think we're going to do a repeat performance as soda jerks. Looking at all that gunk at six o'clock this morning was really more than I could ever take again."

"Yeah, I think in the future we're going to leave the ice-cream-sundae making to some poor man or woman at TD's. They get paid to put those things together for you."

Stevie pretended to be offended by the fact that her friends didn't share her taste in sundaes. It was a joke she was very comfortable with, and so were they. In fact, she was feeling totally comfortable just being with her friends—as if the recent apartness had made her less than whole, and now, like Humpty-Dumpty, she was all back together again.

Something about that reminded her of the story Mrs.

Reg had told her on the way to the hospital—about the two horses who'd been separated. In a way it applied to The Saddle Club, too, as if it had been about three horses instead of two. Being together with her friends made Stevie more than she was when she was alone, and certainly more than she was when she was trying to be something she wasn't, like perfect. When she was with Lisa and Carole, all she ever had to be was Stevie. That was good enough for them, and that was good enough for her.

She wanted to tell Carole and Lisa some of what she'd been thinking. Maybe there was a way to make them understand how much their friendship meant to her.

"You know, I've been thinking," she began. "It's about you two and The Saddle Club."

"Uh-oh, Stevie's sounding serious," Lisa interrupted.

"Definitely time to get her to TD's," Carole said. "She needs a sundae fix."

"Right you are," Stevie agreed. "That sundae this morning just had vanilla frozen yogurt. I've been thinking all day about how much better the whole thing would have been with banana-nut-fudge ice cream."

There were some things you just didn't have to say to real friends. They knew it all anyway.

About the Author

BONNIE BRYANT is the author of more than sixty books for young readers, including novelizations of movie hits such as *Teenage Mutant Ninja Turtles®* and *Honey, I Blew Up the Kid*, written under her married name, B. B. Hiller.

Ms. Bryant began writing The Saddle Club in 1986. Although she had done some riding before that, she intensified her studies then and found herself learning right along with her characters Stevie, Carole, and Lisa. She claims that they are all much better riders than she is.

Ms. Bryant was born and raised in New York City. She lives in Greenwich Village with her two sons.